Cupside Down

TERRY CLIETT

WESTBOW
P R E S S®
A DIVISION OF THOMAS NELSON
& ZONDERVAN

This is a work of fiction. All of the characters, names, incidents, organizations, and dialogue in this novel are either the products of the author's imagination or are used fictitiously.

Unless otherwise noted, all Scripture quotations are taken from the Holman Christian Standard Bible®, Copyright © 1999, 2000, 2002, 2003, 2009 by Holman Bible Publishers. Used by permission. Holman Christian Standard Bible®, Holman CSB®, and HCSB® are federally registered trademarks of Holman Bible Publishers.

WestBow Press books may be ordered through booksellers or by contacting:

WestBow Press
A Division of Thomas Nelson & Zondervan
1663 Liberty Drive
Bloomington, IN 47403
www.westbowpress.com
1 (866) 928-1240

ISBN: 978-1-5127-7236-4 (sc)
ISBN: 978-1-5127-7237-1 (hc)
ISBN: 978-1-5127-7235-7 (e)

Library of Congress Control Number: 2017900783

Print information available on the last page.

WestBow Press rev. date: 01/26/2017

Acknowledgement and Thank You

I suppose no author ever wrote a book without some level of help. Our loving God, no doubt, inspired and directed the writing of this one. I am so thankful for His guidance, and hope I faithfully wrote what He desired to have printed.

So many people have helped me with this book that I will never be able to name or thank them all. I am so thankful to my wife, Sandy, and my son, Elijah, for proofreading and editing for me. I appreciate your time.

A special thank you to my daughter, Emilie, for the cover art. You did an excellent job!

Angie, Glenn, and David, you all helped more than you know. I thank you with my whole heart.

Foreword

The Jonathan Timms in this story is a fictitious character. However, some of the young men I have mentored in the last few years will easily recognize events in the story as true moments in their lives. Although most of this story happened only in the mind of the author, some of the events and people are real.

The events in Chapter 3: Jimmy and the Prison Graduation actually happened in 2015 at a graduation of The Integrity Project® in a prison in Georgia. Only the name of the speaker changed. Terry Cliett delivered the graduation speech that day. They used the Castles of Character© curriculum, which can be ordered from http://www.incorva.com.

Rev. David Self truly does have a coffee house ministry. His book, Everything I Know about Evangelism I Learned at a Coffee House, is available for download.

Many friends and family members gave me suggestions for names or personality traits of characters. Only the characters of Angie and Emilie are true to the real-life people in name and character.

Contents

Chapter 1   This Mess 1

Chapter 2   Jonathan Learns More About Breaches 14

Chapter 3   Jimmy and the Prison Graduation 21

Chapter 4   Jonathan Meets Angie 29

Chapter 5   CIRCLE-F; Temptation 36

Chapter 6   Starting to Build 44

Chapter 7   The Distraction 57

Chapter 8   I-beam 70

Chapter 9   Hope for Ashleigh 81

Chapter 10 New Dance Partner 89

Chapter 11 New Life Plans 102

Chapter 12 What Next? 113

Chapter 13 Rain and DVD 121

Chapter 14 Unfolding Future 129

Chapter 15 Date Surprises 138

Chapter 16 What Happened 147

Chapter 17 Picking up the Pieces 156

Chapter 18 Sum it Up 164

Chapter 1

This Mess

The metal bed frame and springs squeaked with Jonathan's every move. He hung his feet off the side and traced the cracks in the floor with the toe of his shoe. The uncomfortable bed and cold jail cell had given him a sleepless night. Light from the cell across the hall made long shadows on the dirty walls. And the smells? Ugh. Through the bars, he could see the clerk's desk at the end of the hall. He stepped closer to get a better look, more out of boredom than curiosity. He quickly looked away when he thought he saw a man with red hair staring back at him. After a few seconds he peeked through the bars again. The man was gone. Had he imagined it? Jonathan hated jail.

Maybe *someone* would be there soon to bail him out of this mess. *This* mess. How many messes had there been? He'd lost count long ago. Now, after his tantrum and arrest, he knew he had to be missing something. Spending the weekend in jail had given him time to sober up and think about his life. How did trouble keep finding him when he tried so hard to hide from it? He had always thought that laws were for the weak, and that being a man meant you had a right to do whatever you wanted—as long as you didn't get caught. Now, he started to wonder if it was normal for a twenty-three-year-old man to have an arrest record so long he couldn't remember it all.

He closed his eyes, tried to relax, and thought of Katie. She always helped him deal with the hard times. She would encourage him. He could talk to her when he—*Katie!* He jerked and opened his eyes wide as

1

he remembered the evening before. The full weight of his actions began to dawn on him. He couldn't believe he had said those things to her and treated her that way. He thought about the way she had looked at him. That picture became a movie that played in his mind again.

Jonathan, Katie and the rest of their normal party group had been drinking and partying downtown. As usual, the more Jonathan drank, the louder he became. His behavior started to annoy some of the other people in the bar and Katie became concerned. She tried to talk to Jonathan, as did some of his other friends. He kept drinking and trying to show his independence.

"I'm grown, and I'll do what I want!" he screamed when they tried to calm him down.

Finally, Katie tried to reason with him privately. "Please, Jonathan," she pleaded. "I love you, and I know you love me. Please calm down and don't drink any more tonight. Do it for me." Everyone close enough could see the love in her eyes and could hear the concern in her voice.

Jonathan's friends and the other partiers near them all grew quiet for a moment waiting to see Jonathan's response. He didn't respond the way any of them expected.

"For you?" Jonathan broke the silence when he raised his voice in anger. Then he shook a beer bottle in her face and said, loud enough for everyone to hear, "You're crazy if you think you'll ever mean more to me than a good drink."

The look of brokenness on Katie's face froze Jonathan. All of the color left her face, and all of the life seemed to leave her. Her eyes began to water and her voice wavered so much she couldn't speak for a moment. Then she answered him softly but firmly.

"I fully understand now. I didn't want to believe it, but finally I do. I know who I really am – or rather, who I am not – to you. Good bye!" She turned and walked out of Jonathan's life.

The rest of Jonathan's evening blurred in his memory as he continued to drink and pretend that he had everything under control. Then, he woke up in this cell.

How could I be so stupid? he asked himself. Then he looked at the floor again, his eyes wet with a fresh wave of tears. *Can I ever fix my life?* Maybe, just maybe, he didn't have it all together as well as he wanted to believe.

Words would never be able to describe how broken he felt inside. He'd really messed up this time. He wished someone could just open his head and pour in some answers. For the first time in his life, he felt ready to listen.

A metal door slammed somewhere down the hall and the sharp noise made him jump. Was someone coming to tell him his bail had arrived? No. Not until Monday morning, at least. Screaming and cursing from down the hall told him someone else had lost his freedom tonight, too. Jonathan wanted to go home, but he dreaded the questions his mother would have. He wished there'd been someone else he could call to arrange bail for him. He knew he'd have to sit through another long lecture, but he really didn't need any help feeling guilty.

An officer paused outside his door and looked at him. He recognized the officer from a previous stay. The officer gazed directly into Jonathan's eyes and said, "You didn't ask, but I'm going to give you some advice. You need to quit trying to get out of the consequences of your lifestyle and get out of the lifestyle itself. You're not on a good path. In just a few minutes, we'll be transporting someone just one year older than you to the state prison intake center. The judge just sentenced him to five years. Last year, he was in the same cell you're in with the same charges you have. I know you're grown and you're making your own decisions. I respect that, but... are we going to be transporting you next?" He left without waiting for an answer.

Jonathan leaned his head back against the wall and closed his eyes again. He wanted to sleep, but he didn't want anything to crawl on him when he did. The bed wasn't comfortable. His mind raced. So many bad choices seemed to be coming back to haunt him. Somehow he dozed several times, but he kept waking up sweating and shaking.

Bright light coming through the window announced the arrival of Monday morning. As the sun rose, Jonathan found his hopes rising, too. Maybe this would be the last time his mom would have to bail him out. If she could get things together quickly, his release would come soon, and he could get to work before he lost too much time. At least he still had his job—for now. For the first time he began to seriously consider the need for change. Maybe he needed to make some real, permanent changes. But what would he change? *How* would he change? Just trying not to get in trouble didn't work. He'd been trying that.

3

A few hours later, he stared out the car window while his mom drove in silence. Silence wasn't really what he expected and he didn't know how to handle it. He was used to her ranting, and he had gotten better at ignoring that. Of course, she would say she was "giving him a talking to," but he had heard it all before. His mother's lectures just made him angry. She always told him the things he did wrong but never gave him real ways to fix them. This time, though, she seemed to be almost as discouraged and hopeless as he was.

Her voice quivered as she began to talk. "Katie came by to see me this weekend. She told me everything that happened. She said that you really scared her and she's going home to her parents. She left her phone and all the gifts you gave her on my table. She doesn't want you to ever call her again. She said you had threatened her for the last time, and it's over forever." She paused for a moment and said, "She means it, Jonathan. It's over."

She didn't say anything for several minutes. Then she looked at him with red, puffy eyes. Katie had looked at him with the same expression. "How much worse can it get before they...before you're...?" She choked back a sob as her voice cracked.

Jonathan didn't know what to say. He looked at her for a long time. Then he dropped his eyes before his tears started, too. They finished the ride without another word.

Jonathan had his phone number transferred to Katie's old phone and discontinued her old number. His phone had quit working after he dropped it in the pitcher of beer, then threw it against the brick wall on the night he was arrested. He grieved the loss of his relationship with Katie. The memory of Katie's words and the look on her face kept replaying in Jonathan's mind. He couldn't imagine anything the prosecutor or judge could do to him that would make him hurt more. The look of pain in his mother's eyes also seemed to twist the knife of guilt he already felt.

Jonathan spent much of his time thinking about changes he needed to make. Days passed and he still had no real answers. He decided not to wait until his court date. His next step would be to talk directly to the prosecutor and discuss his options.

Whatever happens, he decided, *I'm going to ask her if she knows anyone I can talk to that can help me turn my life around.* He picked up his cell phone and dialed the prosecutor's office.

Two days later he found himself sitting alone waiting in prosecutor Margie Brown's office. Past experience had taught him that he could trust her to be fair, so he chose not to have an attorney this time. He and Ms. Brown had known each other for a long time. He had been in this office so many times to answer for mistakes he had made. While he waited, he noticed she had some new pictures on the wall and a new stapler. The uncomfortable chair he sat in needed replacing, too.

When she finally came in to see him, he expected a lecture like he had gotten before, or even that she'd tell him she had finally given up on him. Maybe he'd have to do some longer jail time or even some prison time for this latest outburst. He was surprised and confused by her response instead. After a brief greeting, she sat down and faced him.

"Well, Jonathan, tell me about this one," she said in a tone that he had heard many times before.

"I seriously want this one to be my last one ever," he responded quickly. "Whatever I have to do to pay for this one, I'm willing to do. I won't fight or argue about it. But I want to know how to change my life and never do this again. I'm tired of jail, and I'm more tired of hurting people I love."

For a good, long time she looked into his eyes across her desk. Her face told the story of the questions she had running through her head. He knew she wondered if he really wanted to change. Finally, she handed him a small piece of paper with a name and phone number on it, and said, "We will discuss what's next after you talk to him."

"Who is this, a counselor or something?" He twisted the corner of his mouth and frowned.

"Or something," she smiled as she answered. "Jimmy Betts can help you get your house in order." When he heard the statement about "getting your house in order" and saw the smile from the prosecutor, Jonathan's train of thought scrambled. The doctor had told his uncle to get his house in order because he only had six months to live. Two of his friends had heard those words just before their report dates. One was reporting for military service, and the other for prison. He didn't ask about his court date or any other details about his charges or sentence. All of the normal questions he might have asked seemed to disappear.

Ms. Brown must have seen that he was confused and speechless. She offered to call and make an appointment for him. The idea of calling a stranger made him uncomfortable, especially when he didn't even know the real reason for the meeting. He agreed to let her set up an appointment for the following morning. He listened while she called.

"Hello, Jimmy," she said after she had dialed the number. "This is Margie. I have a young man in my office that really needs to talk to someone. He's been in a little trouble, and he says he is ready to make some changes. I have several options, but I'd like to send him to you. If you will help him get his house in order, that will take a load off my mind. Will you be available tomorrow?"

She looked at Jonathan and silently mouthed, "Nine o'clock in the morning?" Jonathan nodded.

"He said he would be there," she continued speaking into the receiver. Thank you Jimmy. He really needs your kind of help. I honestly wanted to send him to you, not to a program or class. Thank you so much!"

She wrote the time on a piece of paper that also had Jimmy's name, his business name and address, and phone number on it. She told him to be sure he called if he decided not to go and needed to change the time for any reason.

He rose from his chair, shook her hand and thanked her, then headed for the elevator. Although he had been in trouble many times before, he had never seen this response from Ms. Brown. He had also never had such feelings of guilt or remorse over the things he had done. Her responses had surprised him almost as much as his mother's. Instead of the normal lecture from his mother, he had gotten a few questions accompanied by a look of pain that he hoped he never saw again. He had really blown it this time, but something in Ms. Brown's voice gave him hope.

While on the elevator leaving her office building, Jonathan replayed the conversation in his mind. What did she mean by "get your house in order?" She usually put him on probation or gave him some list of things to complete by some deadline. This time she did neither. He finally decided she must be recommending an attorney or substance abuse counselor. He didn't think he needed either one, but he decided to keep the appointment anyway. As he walked outside his phone buzzed. When he checked it he saw a text from his mom.

"How'd it go?" she had asked, and before he typed a response he realized he had no idea what his options were or what his sentence would be, and never even thought to ask.

"Weird! I'll know more and can tell you about it after a meeting tomorrow. Seems good, though," he replied. He put his phone back into his pocket as he got into his truck. Maybe he'd have real answers tomorrow.

* * *

Jonathan slept well that night but awoke early the next morning. A full hour before his alarm clock went off he stood at his closet trying to decide which shirt to wear. After a shower and a quick breakfast, he drove to the address on the business card for his meeting. Jonathan turned into the parking lot of the small office complex a few minutes early. He noticed a police car in front of the office where he was going. It was parked next to a cleaning service van. Goosebumps ran up his arms and the back of his neck. He shivered. He felt sick. He fought the urge to turn around and leave. A thought flashed across his mind. *She really meant that I needed someone to keep my house in order because I'm going to prison! The police are picking me up and the man I'm meeting is going to get someone to maintain my house while I'm there.* For a few seconds he felt lightheaded. He might have even felt betrayed, if he could've gotten his thoughts together through the panic. All of these thoughts flashed in his mind in less than a second.

Then he saw that the logo on the side of the van matched the logo on one of the office doors. He realized that it belonged to one of the businesses in the office complex. When two police officers came out of the lawyer's office next-door to Jonathan's destination and left, he relaxed a little. Jonathan switched his truck off and ran his hands over his face. Man, he really needed to make some changes. The prison option might be in his future if he didn't change, but nothing he had done so far would result in prison. Why would he even think that?

Since he had arrived a few minutes early, Jonathan took a minute to collect his thoughts and calm down. Those thoughts about prison had come and gone quickly, but still left him nervous. Ms. Brown had seemed so positive and encouraging yesterday. *I am trying to change,* he thought to himself, *and I think she knew it. Nothing bad is waiting for me inside.* When he finally calmed down and convinced himself that Ms. Brown had his best interest in mind when she sent him here, he opened the truck door.

A glass door with a company logo on it gave Jonathan his last pause before he entered the office. The logo had blue letter "I" resting on four blocks with a blue circle around it. The sign said, "The Integrity Project®." Inside, Jonathan found a large but simple waiting room that smelled of fresh coffee. Sitting in a chair at the desk in the far corner, a man looked up from his computer. His graying beard and nearly bald head accompanied a smile that immediately set Jonathan at ease.

"You must be Jonathan," he said as he offered his hand.

"Yes, sir." Jonathan shook his hand and noted the firm grip and the way the man looked him straight in the eye. He almost felt more like an equal in a business deal than someone referred for correction.

"I'm Jimmy Betts. Ms. Brown called and told me to expect you. She said you might need to talk to someone."

Jonathan noticed that Mr. Betts' shirt had the same logo on the left side of his chest and only his first name on the right. He decided that he must prefer that, and made a mental note to call him Jimmy.

"Have a seat, and let's talk a few minutes," Jimmy invited.

Something in Jimmy's tone ignited a spark of hope in Jonathan. Maybe Jimmy had a program or some advice to offer that he hadn't considered at all. *Did Ms. Brown think he might have answers that will help me turn my life around?* Jonathan wondered. The events of the last few days – and the thought of winding up in prison – had scared him enough to make him open to new possibilities.

"Yeah, I guess I do need someone to talk to. I seem to keep making decisions that make other people mad." For a few seconds, Jonathan silently debated with himself about being totally honest with this stranger. He remembered the look on his mother's face, and the look on Katie's face the last time he saw her. Those pictures, and the picture of him in prison, kept running through his mind. He got very still as he stared at his feet. He wrinkled his brow and started breathing faster. Then he continued, "I have an anger problem, and sometimes I make decisions in the heat of the moment that have bad consequences. No matter how much I tell myself I'm going to do better next time, I keep making mistakes and I keep getting in trouble!" He inhaled deeply and continued, "I need someone to tell me how to do better."

"No, you really don't." Jimmy's quick answer caught Jonathan by surprise and left him speechless. After a brief pause, Jimmy continued, "Jonathan, you don't need someone to *tell* you how to *DO* better, you need someone to *teach* you how to *BE* better."

For a long time, he sat quietly trying to figure out the difference between the two statements. He didn't understand the answer, and when he didn't understand something he felt ignorant and out of control. Being out of control made him feel afraid, and fear made him angry. His pulse raced and his face began feel hot.

Once again, he sat talking to someone who knew the rules and the answers. Once again, someone withheld answers that would help him. Anger swelled up in him. Anger ruled his life the way alcohol had ruled his parents' lives in his early childhood. Frustration loomed over his successes and accomplishments. No matter what he did, he missed some important rule or restriction. It seemed he always had to figure them out for himself. Confusion swirled in Jonathan's head. Why wouldn't someone tell him all the rules so he could keep them?

After a few moments, Jimmy continued. "Jonathan, how many times in your adult life has someone told you how to do better? It could have been your parents, or law enforcement, or some friend. How many times?"

Jimmy's tone of voice and the concern in his eyes caught Jonathan's attention. The unpleasant realization registered with Jonathan that he had heard the answers. Many answers. He heard some of them several times. But he kept getting in trouble or somehow getting off track. He found himself considering the ocean of things he did *not* know.

"People are telling me those things all the time. I guess I'm just too stupid to learn." The dark gloominess of despair seemed to close in around him. The room seemed to grow darker and the air somehow seemed to be heavier.

"Stupid? You can learn other things, can't you?" He pointed at Jonathan's phone and said, "You have a nice phone. Were you born knowing how to use it, or did you learn?"

"But…" Jonathan started, then caught himself. Wait. He could learn. He learned to play video games. He could learn in the courses he had taken in college. He could learn the rules for his job at work. He had just learned to cook a new recipe. Maybe he had just not heard the right things. As this awareness grew, he heard Jimmy start to speak again.

"You're not stupid. In fact, I sense that you're pretty smart. That's exactly my point. You don't need someone to tell you what to do. Your need is deeper than that. You need someone to teach you who to be. You need to work on your personal integrity."

9

"Okay," Jonathan said. "Integrity is doing the right thing even when nobody is looking, right? But how do I do that? I've already been trying to do better. *What else can I do?*" The higher pitch of his voice and the slight increase in volume highlighted his frustration.

"I teach classes on personal integrity. It not about what you do as much as who you are. Sometimes Ms. Brown sends people to those classes to help them. But, this time, she sent you to *me*, and not just to a class. I want to help you, Jonathan. I want to help you be the right person, not just try to do the right stuff. I'm willing to pour my life into you. But listen, I don't want to pour my life into you if you're going to turn your cup upside down and waste what I'm offering. This won't be a short class. You need to look at this as a long journey with a distant destination. Or, better yet, think of this as you building your House of Integrity or your Castle of Character."

House of Integrity. Get your house in order. Jonathan was beginning to connect the dots. "Is that what Ms. Brown meant when she said you could 'help me get my house in order'?"

Jimmy laughed. "Probably. I can give you the tools, the information, but you'll have to build the house yourself. Only you can build the house of your personal integrity."

The office phone rang, and Jimmy went to answer it. Jonathan thought about what they had been talking about. No other man had ever had told Jonathan that he would be willing to pour his life into him. Jonathan began to feel a connection with this man who had been a stranger just an hour ago. When Jimmy returned, Jonathan had a response ready.

"Jimmy, I promise," he started to say with moist eyes reflecting his seriousness. "I promise that if you pour your life into me, I won't waste it. I will try. You have my permission to push me, and I will appreciate it. I'm tired of not listening, of turning my cup bottom up when people are trying to help." He sniffled, wiped the corner of his eye, and offered his hand. "How do I start?"

Jimmy shook his hand and said, "*We* start with a cup of coffee. This way to the break room." Jonathan followed him as he walked through the doorway.

Jonathan had tried coffee at several different places over the last few years, but none had been good enough to ever try a second cup. He had almost decided he just didn't like coffee. Even when his mother got the new coffee maker last year and had him try her "new blend," he didn't want a refill. In fact, whatever she had made almost convinced him never to try coffee again. But, since he enjoyed the conversation and his newfound sense of hope so much, he decided to try the coffee here. Maybe it wouldn't be too bad, and he did enjoy talking with Jimmy.

The break room turned out to be more of a break area at the back of a classroom. They entered the room near a screen that looked almost like a movie theatre screen to Jonathan. He later found it stretched over eight feet from corner to corner. Tables set up in a U-shape had about 20 chairs evenly spaced around the outside and facing the screen. A small gap in the center of the setup gave access to the coffee and snack area in the back of the room.

Jimmy's cup looked like it had been waiting for him all morning. His invitation to "grab yourself a cup" started Jonathan on a search. Instead of the sleeve of foam cups that Jonathan expected, he found a selection of other cups. A single foam cup closest to the coffee creamer caught his attention and he reached for it. The green color inside the white cup made Jonathan pause. Jimmy laughed.

"Yeah, you probably don't want that one. We put plant food in that one for the plants near the front windows. I don't think it would hurt you but it might taste like fertilizer." Jonathan smiled briefly as he thought about his mother's coffee and put the cup back.

On the counter right next to the plant food cup sat twin mugs. Well, they might have been twins. At least, they had the same colors. And they might have been mugs at one time. One sat without a handle. The other lay on the table as a neat pile of four pieces. He guessed that someone had dropped them and he wondered why they were still on the counter. Someone should've thrown them away. That made three unusable cups. The one with the hole in the side and the one with the crushed bottom that wouldn't stand up were trash, too, he decided. He counted five unusable cups.

His choices came down to the last two almost identical cups. There was one that appeared to have a crack in the handle and didn't seem dependable and another that looked and felt fine. From all the cups available to him, he only chose the last one. Within a couple of seconds, he had looked at all of the cups and made his decision.

Something about Jimmy captivated Jonathan. He had only met him a few minutes ago and already he felt closer to him than he did to his own father. He loved his father, but he had never known him to be sober.

But this man showed honest concern for him, and somehow that made Jonathan feel like he had value as a real person.

The freshly brewed coffee smelled so good. Jimmy said he had just ground the coffee for this pot a few minutes ago and had just finished brewing it. The sound of the coffee in the cup seemed to call Jonathan by name, and he looked at the bubbles as Jimmy handed him the cup. He held it up and smelled the rich aroma before he took a sip. It tasted so good!

Jonathan wondered how long it would be before Jimmy would begin teaching him. He didn't have to wait long for an answer. Jimmy motioned for him to sit down and asked him about his coffee cup selection.

"What made you pick that particular cup?"

Jonathan thought about his answer for a moment before he said, "It was the only good cup over there." He got no immediate response, so he continued. "Your cup was there, but it wouldn't have been good to take your cup since you had already been using it. The plant watering cup would've made the coffee taste bad so it wasn't good, either."

"But what about the other cups?"

"There were no other good cups. One had no handle, and another was broken. One had a hole in it and the sides looked too thin. One had a messed up bottom and wouldn't sit flat on the table. The only other one over there looked like it might break and spill coffee at any time. I picked the only good cup."

"So, what you're telling me is that two of the cups wouldn't hold good coffee. One would have my germs in it and another would have plant food in it. Right?"

Jonathan squirmed a little and started to answer. He didn't want to be rude, but the germ issue had crossed his mind. And no one wants to drink plant food.

Jimmy continued without giving him a chance to respond. "The cup without a handle missed the mark because a piece was missing. You wanted a whole cup. The broken one missed the mark because it had all the parts, but none in the right places. You wanted a complete cup. The one with the hole in it and weak sides might not hold coffee. You wanted a solid cup. The one with the crushed bottom lacked the soundness or the stability you wanted. You didn't choose the one with the cracked handle because you wanted a dependable cup. Am I right on all this?"

Jonathan wondered how much time Jimmy had spent setting up the cups and the entire coffee scene. "Yes, sir."

"What you're really saying is that you wanted a cup with integrity. You wanted it to be good, whole, complete, solid, sound, and dependable. You wanted it to have all of those qualities, to be all of those things. That is the definition of integrity. You chose the cup you're using now because it was a good cup. That meant it would meet its potential – hold coffee."

"I just wanted it to be a cup." Jonathan's answer sounded short and almost rude. He understood, but wondered why they had spent so much time talking about the cup instead of the coffee. And what did this have to do with him getting his house in order?

"Don't you see, Jonathan? Your family and friends don't want you to do all the right things or not do all of the wrong things. They just want you to *be* Jonathan. The good, whole, complete, solid, sound, and dependable Jonathan that they know you can be and were always meant to be. If your integrity is intact, your behavior will show it. It's all about integrity. You don't want a cup that is broken or has a breach of any kind. And you don't try to pour coffee in it with the bottom up. Remember the cup."

For the next hour they talked about coffee, the weather, when they would meet again, and generally just passed the time. When they could endure the hard chairs in the classroom no more, they stood and stretched. They washed their cups and set them aside for the next time.

The sun seemed brighter and the grass seemed greener as Jonathan walked across the parking lot to his truck. He didn't know whether to credit the caffeine in the coffee or the content of the conversation, but somehow he just felt better.

Chapter 2

Jonathan Learns More About Breaches

After a partial day at work, Jonathan spent some time at his mother's house. It took a couple of hours to tell her about his latest adventures with the prosecutor and with Jimmy. Jonathan explained the concept of integrity and told her about the coffee cups. He could tell by the look on her face that she still worried about him.

"Don't worry, Mom," Jonathan reassured her. "I really am going to change. I don't want to hurt you anymore. I think Jimmy might be able to help me."

"I hope so," she said. She started to say something else, but stopped. Jonathan hugged her. She looked tired and worried to him.

"I have to work tomorrow, and you have things to do, so I'm going home now," Jonathan said. He kissed her on the forehead. "I'll see you soon. Don't worry!" He hugged her again and stepped out the door.

"Okay, I'll try!" she said and tried to smile. She waved as Jonathan cranked his truck and drove away.

He arrived at his apartment just after sunset. He stood for a few minutes enjoying the bright orange sky and the deepening blue of the clouds. In those remaining moments of daylight, a deserted lawn mower near the edge of the parking lot caught his attention. Immediately his mind flashed back to the landscape equipment he had seen that morning. For a few fleeting moments he had considered the possibility that he might go to prison. That two-second memory from the morning made him shiver again.

The goosebumps rode his back all the way to his front door and into his living room. He retreated to the comfort of his sofa, but forgot to turn on his television or the lights. Sitting in the silent darkness of the living room, he meditated on his life. He had made so many mistakes and hurt so many people. Now he had totally lost the relationship with the woman he loved and had planned to marry. Change had to start, and start now. When the growling of his stomach interrupted his thoughts, he looked around. The only lights were the little beacons on the cable box and on the clock on the microwave in the kitchen.

He walked slowly toward the refrigerator to get something to eat. As he turned on the light in the kitchen, he realized he was still wearing his work shoes. He always left them by the front door to keep from tracking mud on the carpet. He couldn't afford to lose his security deposit because of some muddy carpets. After slipping off his shoes and placing them near the doorway to the living room, he washed his hands.

Two sandwiches and a glass of milk later he started thinking about going to bed. He'd have a full day of work tomorrow and that meant getting up early. He looked at the hole in the toe of his left sock and hoped he had a clean pair in his room. All of his clean clothes were in two baskets in the floor. One day, he decided, he'd start folding his clean clothes and keeping them in the drawers. But not today.

As he started to get undressed, he noticed the hole again. "Sock, you have lost your integrity," he laughed as he threw it away. Integrity in socks, integrity in coffee cups, integrity in people. His talk with Jimmy had that word stuck in his mind. He had always thought of himself as a good person, but the events of the last few days had convinced him to take another look. He could see where his personal integrity had some holes in it. He stretched out on the bed and reached for the lamp. He started dreaming almost before the room got fully dark.

Jonathan's phone rang a full hour before he had planned to get up the next morning. The voice on the other end belonged to his boss from work, who also happened to be his Uncle Steve. Uncle Steve sounded intense and serious. Jonathan jumped out of bed.

Jonathan had worked with his uncle, Steve Green, since he turned fifteen. Uncle Steve had more patience than most men did and he had a special passion for helping young people. He looked like the loving uncle in appearance and attitude. Uncle Steve called himself a "middle man." He'd say, "I'm a middle man. I'm middle aged and medium height. I'm round in the middle and always in the middle of doing something." Most of the time being in the middle of something meant mentoring a young person. He gave Jonathan a chance to work and learn under patient supervision.

Working after school and on weekends, Jonathan learned to drive and operate both the tractor and the backhoe his first year. Then he learned to use the other heavy equipment before he turned 20. Uncle Steve gave him enough time off to take some classes at the local college and made allowances for Jonathan's brushes with the law, partly because of his abilities, and partly because of their family relationship. Jonathan really knew how to run a backhoe, and that skill mattered to everyone today.

"Get dressed and come on in, Son," Uncle Steve started. "The sheriff just called and said the rains from upstream have caused Lake Stuart to overrun. They found a breach in the Lake Stuart dam. Before a small situation becomes a huge problem, we need to move. I'll have our backhoe there when you get there. We're closer than anyone else. The sheriff says we might have another Earl. You know what that means."

Jonathan did know what that meant. Just four years ago, Lake Earl's dam had a breach. That 20-acre lake reminded him of Lake Stuart. Both were about the same size, and many would call them ponds instead of lakes. Still, they held too much water to be released suddenly. The flat land behind the dam would surely be flooded.

While the local officials had tried to decide what to do at Lake Earl, the breach had deepened and widened until the whole dam gave way. From drip to deluge had taken less than a day. All the water came rushing downstream, wiped out the old Marshville schoolhouse, and flooded acres of farmland. No one died or suffered any personal harm, but the area changed forever. He had read that the property damage totaled over two million dollars.

A similar thing might happen again. Downstream from Lake Stuart, four houses and a church building would be in danger of flooding. Jonathan knew that repairing a breach quickly helps prevent tragedies, so he wasted no time. He also knew that his uncle's company might have already been finished with a retaining wall that would protect the church, and maybe the houses, if Jonathan hadn't taken his most recent jail adventure. In simple terms, if the dam broke he would feel like the damages to the houses and church were his fault. He hurried as quickly as he could to meet Uncle Steve.

When Jonathan arrived on the jobsite, he saw a tall man with an orange hardhat stood holding a clipboard standing just in front of Uncle Steve. Uncle Steve had already unloaded the backhoe and motioned to Jonathan to join them. After a very quick introduction, engineer John Winters started telling Jonathan what to do before he could finish saying hello. Mr. Winters asked Jonathan no questions and left no time for Jonathan to ask him any. He gave direct instructions that made it sound to others as if he and Jonathan had been working together for years. What he said and the way he said it made perfect sense to Jonathan, and he wasted no time. Two hours later, they were finished and ready to load the backhoe onto the trailer.

"Good job!" Mr. Winters told Jonathan when he finished. "I like to catch problems like this when they're small and easy to fix. Since it rained upstream yesterday, we didn't have much time." He paused while a red-headed man handed Jonathan some tools and a piece of chain that had been on the trailer with the backhoe. Jonathan thought the man looked familiar, but his attention went back to Mr. Winters as he continued talking. "We caught it just right so it didn't take long. I'm glad I was in the area. You're pretty good with that machine. You must be a big help to your uncle." Jonathan shook hands with him and got in the truck to go get breakfast. Uncle Steve would bring the trailer and backhoe with him later.

Jonathan had never really thought about the things he did as actually helping his uncle. He only thought about doing his work and getting a paycheck. He called Chelsea at the office to let her know where he had been. Uncle Steve had been at the lake, but Chelsea kept track of the work assignments and answered the phone in the office. Her scheduling skills and phone skills made her a fair receptionist, but sometimes she talked too fast and too much. Her habit of gossiping about people meant he needed to give her only basic information. Anything more and she'd begin the gossip chain. He only told her that he'd be stopping for breakfast before going to his next worksite. Then he parked at Aunt Jo's Diner and went in to eat.

Jonathan, and most of the local work crews in town, ate at Aunt Jo's Diner at least once a week. The small building that had the "Aunt Jo's Diner" sign in the front window had been many things, but few people could remember the fried chicken or the ice cream part of its history. Most people could only remember the home-cooking diner that felt so much like home. Almost everyone called the owner Aunt Jo or Auntie Jo. But other than her daughter, Joy, Jonathan didn't know anyone actually related to her.

The new girl stood ready to take his order before he got to his table. Sixteen-year-old Kayla had introduced herself to him the last time he came in for breakfast. Aunt Jo bragged about how much she helped them and everyone really liked her. Kayla asked Jonathan if he wanted his usual and he said yes. Then, she and her cute smile disappeared in the breakfast crowd. He had to admit that what people had said about her seeming like their favorite younger sister proved true. The look in his eyes and his slight smile projected his satisfaction. Kayla really had made him feel welcomed and gave him a sense of belonging.

Wait! Jonathan thought as he watched her weave through the crowd toward the kitchen. *She hasn't been here long, and I've only been in here one other time when she took my order. How does she know what my usual order is?* Did she have a crush on him? She was only sixteen and he really didn't think that was it. Still, he was curious. How did she know? Had Aunt Jo or Joy told her? He made up his mind to ask her when she returned.

She brought the plate of eggs, bacon, and toast and the glass of juice all prepared just the way he liked them. Her humble tone and sparkling eyes added sweetness to her question, "Did I get it right?"

"Yes!" he answered a little louder and more energetically than he intended. Then he softened his voice to ask, "But, how did you know?"

"When Aunt Jo and Joy interviewed me, they said they needed help. But they didn't need help just taking orders and serving food. They needed help loving the people they thought about as family. They asked me if I could help them love their family, their customers, by helping in the dining room. That's what I really wanted to do. So I just think of everyone as family, and try to remember what they like. Sometimes I get it wrong, but I try. I think about it like I'm helping Aunt Jo and helping the family – you know, the customers."

Kayla seemed to feel satisfaction in her work because she had purpose. She was helping Aunt Jo, Joy, and the customers. She seemed to see herself as having a purpose, so she recognized her own value to the restaurant and to the customers. Jonathan was beginning to feel the same way about his job. Why had he not recognized this before?

For the rest of the day, he thought about his work as something he did to help his uncle. He began to pay closer attention to the details of his work. Thinking about helping Uncle Steve made his job more personal than it had been before. Working on heavy equipment loud enough to block out other noise gave Jonathan plenty of time to think.

Today, he had many things on his mind. This new sense of personal value excited him. He could actually make a difference in other people's lives. He WAS making a difference in other people's lives! He even began to think about the people his uncle contracted with for the work. They also needed his help. He had never thought of himself as important in that way before. He had to smile as he parked the tractor and headed for home. The engineer and the pretty young waitress had taught him something today.

On his way to his apartment, Jonathan thought about the work on the dam that morning. The engineer said they had restored the "structural integrity" of the dam. That word "integrity" kept popping up. The dam had a breach so it had lost its integrity. His work had restored its integrity, repaired the breach, and saved property and livestock. It could have even saved lives, but he might never know about that. He did know that it had been a long day and that it felt good to be home.

When he had wiped his boots on the grass and his doormat, he pulled them off. He opened the door and placed his boots in their usual spot near the door in one motion. The orange light of the setting sun filtered through the window in the kitchen. He thought about how easy it had been to take off his boots and how hard it would be to take off bad habits. He laughed to himself. If only you could take off your breaches like you take off your britches!

He sat down to eat the leftovers his mother had sent to him and began to think. His head felt like a movie theatre with two screens showing at the same time. One screen played his breaches that had gotten him in trouble lately. The other screen played all the possible things his friends would be doing out on the town tonight. He got a chill when he realized that both screens were playing the same movie.

Those activities with his friends had resulted in his jail time. His mother kept saying that he hung out with the wrong crowd. The deep realization of his mother's error almost made him choke on his meatloaf. *I'm not hanging out with the wrong crowd. I AM the wrong crowd!* He had a new focus for his next talk with Jimmy. He knew how to do wrong things; he hoped Jimmy could tell him how to *un*-do wrong things.

Chapter 3

Jimmy and the Prison Graduation

Graduation for the Integrity Dorm at Hardison State Prison started at 10:00 a.m. Inmates on the Integrity Dorm studied the *Castles of Character*© material that Jimmy Betts had written. When they completed the course, the prison sponsored a graduation and allowed them to invite their families. As always, Jimmy Betts arrived a half hour early. He knew that the process of going through the checkpoints took time. He double-checked his pockets as he crossed the hot parking lot. A cell phone, pocketknife, or any other contraband in his pocket when he entered the prison could get him a five-year sentence. His hand reached to his belt for the third time to be sure he didn't have his cell phone. He checked his pocket to be sure he had his identification cards. Then he opened the door to the entrance.

"Hello, Mr. Betts," a corrections officer said as soon as he entered. She recognized him because he had been coming for over eleven years. "How are you today?"

"Getting better, Ms. Atchison," he answered, smiling.

She returned his smile, and replied, "I really like how you always say that. I think I'm going to start using that."

He signed in and began to remove his shoes and the contents of his pockets. He put them in a small basket and placed them on a conveyor belt that carried them through an x-ray machine. Then he walked through the metal detector and gave Ms. Atchison his identification card. When he put his shoes back on, he went through the next door and onto a walkway. After another officer remotely opened a number of locked gates and doors for him, he arrived at the visitation room. The room held a podium, sound system, and chairs for the graduates and visitors. It looked just like the last graduation a few months ago. Many of the inmates recognized him from the video they had studied. Some smiled and waved at him.

The Deputy Warden, Mr. Aubrey Williams, immediately noticed him and started toward him with a smile. He spoke of the changes in the inmates and the atmosphere on the dorm. Chaplain Meeks approached and shook Jimmy's hand. She had known Jimmy for over twenty years, and they were friends. At one time he had been her pastor. Other staff and previous graduates of the program waved at him or spoke briefly to him as they passed by. Some of the inmates' families had already found seats and others looked for theirs. Most of them looked excited and a little nervous.

Jimmy heard a man whisper to his wife, "I hope this program really does help him change." The man turned toward Jimmy and extended his hand. "Are you the Mr. Betts that my son told me about? The man who wrote this program?"

"I am," Jimmy smiled as he answered and shook the man's hand.

"I'm Herbert Smart, and my son is graduating today. He has liked the program, and I really hope that it works for him," he said. The emotion in his voice and the look in his eyes told Jimmy that the man loved his son and desperately wanted him to change.

"If he wants to change," Jimmy replied, "this will be a good set of tools for him to use. Many people have changed their lives using this as a blueprint."

Jimmy had been a prison chaplain at another prison when he wrote the first draft of the program material. Since then, he had revised the material over a dozen times before developing the video and student books that the prison now used. In the last twelve years, he had spoken at the graduations of over 2,000 participants. He always looked forward to these occasions. The inmates always blessed him with their stories of life changing revelations and decisions. His personal sacrifices began to seem tiny in comparison with hope that glowed in the eyes of these graduates and their families.

One of the chaplain's aides gave Jimmy a graduation program and showed him to his "seat of honor" near the podium. While everyone took their seats, the lights in the room were adjusted and the doors closed. Jimmy began to daydream. For a moment, his mind went back in time to one of the first classes he had taught in the prison setting. Fourteen years ago he had been the chaplain when he taught the course. One of the inmates had been paying particularly close attention. Near the beginning of the second night of class, he made a strong statement.

"Chaplain, my family is the most important thing in the world to me. No matter what, I won't sacrifice my family," he had said very strongly.

"That's a good core value, and holding to that will help you be a person of Integrity," he had told the man. Although Jimmy wondered why someone so committed to his family had wound up in prison, he didn't ask. Maybe the man had decided after he entered prison that his priorities needed to change. The follow-up statement the man had made at the end of the course ten weeks later would ring in Jimmy's ears for many years.

"Chaplain, you remember when I told you at the beginning of the course that my family was the most important thing in the world to me?" he asked near the end of the course.

"Yes, I do," Jimmy had answered.

"Well," the man continued, "I remember my wife sent me to the store one time to buy diapers for my little girl, and I came back home with beer instead." He paused briefly as tears began to form in his eyes. "Chap, I throwed away my little girl for that alcohol, didn't I?"

Jimmy noticed the regret in the man's eyes that began to ride the tears down his cheeks. Jimmy had no choice but to answer honestly, "Yes, you did."

Tears ran like rivers down the man's cheeks as he spoke slowly and clearly through clenched teeth. "Never again!" he said with obvious anger and resolve. "Chap, I'm in prison for habitual violator – DUI. I have had every stop-drinking class the state has to offer. I know how to stop drinking. But until now, no one ever told me *why* to stop drinking. My little girl is why, and I will *never* drink again." He pounded the desk lightly but firmly with his fist as he finished the statement.

Jimmy would never forget that moment. And there had been others through the years. Jimmy's mind returned to the present graduation, and he wondered what stories he might hear today. He looked at the program the chaplain's aide had given him and began to read.

The program held a surprise: two of the inmates had written a rap using the course content and would perform it. Three others would talk about what the program had meant to them as a closing after Jimmy's address. He briefly thought about Jonathan. Maybe Jonathan would be humble enough to learn before he wound up in one of these striped uniforms. Many others had changed course and avoided prison. Some did not.

As Jimmy looked at the audience, many of the inmates looked at him and smiled or nodded. They all wore the white prison uniform that had the blue stripe down each leg. Jimmy noted how clean and pressed each uniform looked; not exactly typical of the average prisoners.

He guessed that about seventy inmates sat in the reserved chairs on the speaker's left. The chairs were in neat rows with about eight chairs in each row. The graduating men were on the front five rows. Behind them sat the other occupants of the dorm, some who had graduated already, some who would be in the next class. One inmate sat in a wheelchair on the end of one of the rows. Standing, in the back of the room behind the inmates, security personnel watched both inmates and visitors.

The visiting family and the staff sat to the speaker's right and waited while talking quietly to one another. Some of the counselors and families talked and seemed to be pointing out certain graduates. Jimmy saw one couple looking and smiling at one of the graduates. The young man waved at them and gave them a "thumbs up."

Jimmy sighed and smiled. He knew that, for some of these men, this graduation marked the first thing in their lives they had ever successfully finished. The ceremony was beginning, so he turned his attention to the podium.

Deputy Warden Williams spoke first. After a few minutes of the expected "greetings on behalf of the Department of Corrections," and the "our warden couldn't be here today but…" statements, he introduced the chaplain.

"Thank you for coming to our graduation ceremony," Chaplain Meeks began. "The men have been working so hard on the curriculum, and some have special presentations ready for today." She turned and looked at Jimmy. "Mr. Betts has been a friend of mine for many years, and I will give him a full introduction in a few minutes, but some of the men have prepared their own introductions to the material they have been studying. We hope you like it."

Chaplain Meeks introduced two young men who had written a rap about the curriculum content. Two younger black members of the graduating class came forward and looked briefly at Jimmy. The taller winked and pointed at Jimmy, the other nodded his head and smiled. Then, they turned toward the audience.

"We have learned a lot while taking this class," the first man said.

"And the definitions were not always easy to learn, so," the second continued.

They both turned toward Jimmy with huge smiles and the first finished the sentence, "We hope you don't mind, Mr. Betts, but we put the words to music in this little rap."

They turned to face the audience again and began, first one, then the other echoed, then together:

"Integrity!"

"Integrity!"

"The quality or state of being good, whole, complete, solid, sound, and dependable. Integrity."

"Integrity!"

"The man I want to be!"

"The quality or state of being good, whole, complete, solid, sound, and dependable. Integrity."

They continued through the rest of the definitions in perfect rhythm. Many of the audience began to nod or bounce to the rhythm of the beat. Jimmy noted that even some of the attending security officers seemed to be bouncing a little.

No one would accuse Jimmy Betts of being a rap music fan. At least, not until these two started. Every single important definition from the *Castles of Character* curriculum stood out in the rap. Jimmy thought as he listened that both men could have passed a test on the content just by what they put in the words of the rap. For the rest of the day, Jimmy imagined how effective this might be if these men could present that to school groups.

The chaplain introduced Jimmy next, so he walked to the podium. Part of Jimmy's address seemed to really catch the attention of the visitors and the staff. "Many times people ask me if the *Castles of Character* program works. The answer is *NO*. Programs don't work, people do. But if a person wants to change, if he really wants to improve himself, *Castles of Character* provides a good toolbox for him to use in building his personal integrity." The inmates had heard this before and applauded in heartfelt agreement.

Jimmy's voice cracked with emotion as he gave his final statement before sitting down. He pointed his finger at the graduates and his voice thundered with passion as he said, "Don't you give up. I believe in you! As long as I live, there will be one person who believes that you can change, that you can make it. Don't quit. You and only you have control of your integrity. From this moment forward, you don't have to be who you were before. You can be a new man with a positive influence on your peers and on your family...on your children. You can do it! Will you?"

He took his seat next to the podium with his knees shaking and his arms quivering. He had poured himself into that final charge. Only after he composed himself for a few seconds did he realize the inmates and their families were applauding. Some of the inmates had tears running down their cheeks. Many of their family members were wiping their noses and eyes.

As the chaplain called out the names of the men, they came forward for their certificates. In single file, they shook hands with Deputy Warden Williams and received their certificates. Jimmy and three prison staff members shook their hands and congratulated them. A diverse group of black, white, Hispanic, and Asian men, ranging in age from early twenties to late sixties, had graduated. When the applause ended, the chaplain offered the microphone to any graduates who wanted to address the group.

Three men gave testimonials. The first speaker, a very round white man in his sixties, walked slowly to the podium and looked at the crowd. He made eye contact with each of the visitors and addressed the quiet room. "You wouldn't believe how much this program has changed me. I'm usually a country music fan, but I now like at least one rap song." He started repeating the rap, shaking his big behind, and imitating the arm motions of the two who had presented earlier. No one heard the words because the room had erupted in laughter.

His eyes glistened as he pointed at the two rappers then bent over and laughed at himself. They pointed back at him and almost fell out of their chairs. Their open-mouthed cackles lost sound in the rush of laughter. In the release of the moment, every one shared a beautiful experience. Here, for the moment, race and age didn't matter. Music choice didn't matter. Past mistakes didn't matter. These men shared a common bond: the desire to be better men for themselves and their families.

When the laughter subsided, the next speaker came forward. "Until I took this course, I didn't know that I had value. I thought that I had given up all of my value when I got convicted and sent to prison. Now that I know that I have value as a person even though I have done wrong things, I'm more free now than I was before I was locked up. I don't know if that makes any sense …" The applause and affirmation from the other inmates drowned out the rest of his sentence.

The final speaker thanked the chaplain, staff, and Mr. Betts for making the program available. "*Castles of Character* has really changed my life. I now know that some of the things my family tried to tell me were true all along." Then he turned toward some of the visitors and said, "I'm truly sorry for who I was and what I did to all of you. I'm not going to make promises to you. I did that before. But I will tell you this: if you watch me, I will show you that I'm a better man." His voice seemed to crack, but he maintained his composure and went to his seat.

The applause died down and the room grew quiet as the chaplain spoke again. "We have refreshments in the back and would like to invite our guests and visitors to go first." The formal ceremony ended and the informal greeting and visiting began.

Many of the participants wanted to shake hands with Jimmy and give him their thanks and best wishes. Some offered emotional stories about how the program had helped them and some gave hollow praise. The statement of one inmate stuck with Jimmy for a long time.

"Mr. Betts," the thin black man in his thirties began, "I didn't have no daddy growing up, and my mama worked all the time trying to do for us. I didn't know what you taught in this class. Watching you on that DVD I could see that you cared and that these things really matter. I'm a changed man. When I get out next year, I want to take what I learned back to my old neighborhood and teach the young men there. There is too much violence and hate in that neighborhood. I believe they will listen to me. At least, some of them will. I want to teach them what you taught me."

"Man, that is so powerful! Thank you for sharing that with me." Jimmy said as he reached out and shook hands with him. "I'm so glad the program helped you. I'm proud of you and proud of your efforts."

"There is something else I'm going to tell them." The inmate said as his gaze focused in Jimmy's eyes. "I'm going to tell them that this race hate and thinking that white people don't care is crap. I'm going to tell them about you, and that a white man told me what I'm telling them, so we have to move on past this hate and learn to get along. We all need integrity. That's what I'm going to tell them." He turned and went to the refreshment table.

It really didn't happen often, but Jimmy Betts had absolutely no words for a response. He always felt humbled by the fact that God had chosen him to write the curriculum, and more so when he got responses like this one. He stood in a silent shock until he heard the chaplain encouraging him to get some cake and punch.

All the way down the halls, through the front gate and back to his car, Jimmy pondered the things he had just seen. He walked slowly as he thought and meditated. Then he realized he had an appointment with Jonathan and picked up his pace.

"If I hurry," he said aloud as he opened his car door, "I might just be on time."

Chapter 4

Jonathan Meets Angie

Jonathan sat in his truck for a couple of minutes before he went in for his meeting with Jimmy. So many thoughts ran through his mind. His friends had been calling and texting him for the last couple of weeks wanting him to go drinking and partying with them. Some seemed like friendly invitations while others were almost bitter and accusing. The old Jonathan would've already been back in the swing of the social activities, but he wanted to change. He knew what the chain of events would be: they would drink and have fun for a while; he'd get mad about something; there would be a fight; he'd wind up in jail.

One text this morning had invited him to an autograph signing party Friday night. Another one accused him of being "too good to hang out with common people anymore" and reminded him that he "would always be stuck here with us." Some of these texts didn't make any sense to him at all. What were they talking about?

He missed the fun and the interaction with his friends but he didn't miss waking up in jail. How many times could you take roaches waking you up by trying to crawl in your ear? Or your cellmate being sick in your shoes? He really hated jail. So, he really had been avoiding most of his friends as much as he could. He planned to stay away from them until he could figure out how to stay out of trouble. That reminded him of what he had really wanted to talk to Jimmy about today. He needed to figure out how to *un*-do some things. He looked forward to talking to Jimmy today. He parked his truck and headed for the door.

The smell of coffee tickled Jonathan's nose even before he opened the door to Jimmy's office. An unexpected female voice greeted him as soon as he stepped inside. "Hello! You must be Jonathan!"

He had expected to see Jimmy sitting at the desk and to hear his voice. Nothing had prepared him for this greeting! He stumbled over his words as he tried to return the greeting. A pretty woman in her late thirties extended her hand. She glowed with a smile that made him feel at once welcome, encouraged, and at peace. Unable to speak, with mouth ajar and a confused frown on his brow, he shook her hand.

"I'm Angie," she explained. "Jimmy told me about you, and he'll be right back. Can I get you some coffee while you wait?" Jonathan felt relieved to learn how she knew his name. The idea of coffee sounded good and she seemed so eager that he immediately accepted the offer. This would be the first time he had ever accepted a second cup of coffee anywhere. He hoped he wouldn't regret it. He also hoped she'd bring some creamer or sugar with her when she brought the coffee. He didn't feel comfortable following her to the back since he hadn't been invited, but he really didn't think he could drink his coffee black.

He saw Jimmy coming to the front door just as Angie handed him the coffee. It looked like she had already put some creamer in it, so he tried it. And he loved it. He stared into the cup and didn't even look up when Jimmy walked through the door.

Jimmy started to laugh. "Angie must have made you some coffee." He said it almost as if it he expected no answer or response. "Angie, you have another convert. I told Jonathan last week that if he really wanted good coffee, he should let you make him a cup. He said he wasn't much of a coffee drinker, though."

"I am now!" Jonathan answered. Then he looked shocked that he had actually said it aloud. They all laughed as Angie stepped back into her office and returned almost immediately with a newspaper.

"I thought you might want copies of this, so I brought you mine. I didn't know whether you had one or not, but I know your mother will want an extra one." Angie smiled and handed him the paper.

Jonathan wondered what might be in the newspaper to make Angie save him a copy, and why she'd think his mother would want one. But, she had made him a cup of coffee so he decided to be polite. He took it and glanced at the front before he started to fold it to look at later. Then he froze. He recognized the hat on the man in the picture on the front. It was *his* hat.

"That's me!" he said. He hadn't thought about it since the day of the work on the dam, but now he remembered seeing a person with a camera. His focus on the dam had kept him from noticing everything else that had been going on that day.

Reading the article brought almost as much surprise as the picture on the front page had. The article mostly contained information about the damage that could have happened if the dam had broken. It listed the places that would've been flooded or suffered major water damage. One section explained the potential damage to crops and livestock. One part even had something about the possible loss of human life. Jonathan shook his head as he read. Fixing the problem had not been nearly as hard as the article made it sound. The caption under the photograph kept calling Jonathan's eyes back to it.

> *Our hero doesn't wear armor and ride a horse; he wears*
> *a baseball cap and rides a backhoe.*

Jonathan stared at the picture for a minute and said to himself, "That's not a picture of a hero. That's just a picture of a jailbird on a backhoe." He dreaded the teasing he'd get from his friends about this. It had already started this morning, but he hadn't known what they meant. Now he understood.

"Why do newspapers have to exaggerate everything?" he asked, not really expecting an answer.

Almost as if exiting a fog, he began to be aware of his surroundings again. He still held his coffee cup, but the small amount of cold coffee told him he had been daydreaming for a long time. When he looked around from his seat on a futon in the office, Jimmy and Angie had gone to their offices. He hoped he hadn't seemed rude. The newspaper article had shocked him so much that he just ignored them and focused on reading.

Angie came near and spoke to him in a cheerful but quiet voice. "Do you need more coffee?" She took his cup before he could answer and disappeared toward the break area. She came back almost immediately with his refill and pointed toward the back of the classroom. "Jimmy is back there if you want to talk to him."

The classroom looked exactly the way he remembered it from a couple of weeks ago, with Jimmy even wearing the same thing. Somehow, though, it felt different. It looked familiar and felt strange at the same time. He hadn't quite decided what to say when Jimmy started to smile.

"Did the coffee do that to you, or did something else scramble your brain?"

Jonathan recognized this as more of an invitation to talk than a question that needed an answer. He began to pour out his confusions and concerns while Jimmy just let him talk.

"I have been having a hard time since the day I did the work on the dam. That newspaper article brought it all back to me. It really exaggerated what I did to the dam. I had no trouble at all doing the work. The engineer told me what to do. It made perfect sense and I did it. That fixed the dam." He sighed and shook his head. "It made me really think about myself. Why is it so easy to fix breaches in *things* and so hard to fix breaches in *yourself*? I have disappointed and hurt so many people. I'm ashamed of it and tired of being me. I want to change it all, but how do you undo the things you've done?"

He paused and looked at Jimmy, who patiently waited for him to continue. Jonathan relaxed his hold on his coffee cup and continued.

"I wanted to have a wife and family, to own my own company, and be a respected person in the community," he said. "Now I'm just a failure, and worse than that, a joke. The newspaper article makes me feel worse, because I know I'm not what it says. And I have hurt…"

Jonathan struggled to keep from breaking down as he recalled the hurt in his mother's eyes when she talked to her friends about him. Then he began to talk about his partying and drinking on the night just before his recent arrest. He couldn't finish his sentence when he spoke about his anger outburst that cost him his relationship with his fiancé.

"And the things I said to her, loud enough for everyone to hear, I just…" he never finished the sentence.

For a long time, he sat broken and silent, with his head down. Then he looked at Jimmy and found himself looking into the eyes of someone who cared. He thought he saw a teardrop on Jimmy's collar. He knew he saw mercy and compassion in his eyes. After waiting just long enough for both of them to be fully composed, Jimmy started to speak.

"Unfortunately you can never undo those things or unsay those words. You didn't un-breach the dam. You repaired it. You may be able to repair the relationships you're talking about after some time has passed, but you cannot undo the actions. You cannot unsay the words. I don't think you realize how much you hurt your mother and your fiancé."

"I think I'm starting to realize it. I did a lot of things that hurt Mom, and Katie, too. I did try to stop hurting them, but I guess I couldn't."

"I don't want to make it seem like I'm fussing at you or being critical," Jimmy began, "but even if you fully understand what you're saying, you only have half of the picture. You didn't just hurt them by what you *did*; you also hurt them by what you *didn't* do."

Jonathan turned in his chair, clasped his hands together, and put them on the table. He felt so confused and frustrated. He had more questions than he could put into words. If he didn't understand how much he had hurt the most important people in his life, he might as well quit. He felt his heartbeat increase and the room seemed to be getting warmer. The muscles in his chest and arms tensed and he started breathing faster. He had to fight the urge to get up and leave.

Jimmy put his hand on Jonathan's shoulder. His tone sounded affirming and challenging at the same time when he said, "You can be angry if you want to. Be angry with me or be angry with yourself. But if you really do care about your mother and Katie, don't leave here until you work through the anger. Then you can start working on your breaches with a clear head."

Jimmy's statements registered in Jonathan's mind as permission to be angry and encouragement to move on through it. The idea that he could work through his anger and get through it with a plan instead of a problem gave Jonathan hope. He relaxed a little.

"You see, Jonathan," Jimmy continued, "breaches in personal integrity can show up in two different ways. One is an active breach. That's when you do something you shouldn't. You actively do wrong. The other is a passive breach. That's when you don't do something you should. You pass up the opportunity to do right. Does that make sense?"

Jonathan calmed down a little more. Now that he had a better understanding of what Jimmy was trying to say, he became less frustrated with the situation. But he became more frustrated with himself for not knowing all this already. His mind flashed back to a situation he had observed between Chelsea and Uncle Steve when she first started working with the company.

Jonathan and Uncle Steve had been working that morning while Chelsea took care of the office. Her responsibilities included cleaning, emptying the wastebaskets, filing, and other general office work.

On this particular day, Uncle Steve had left her some money and asked her to order lunch for herself, him, and Jonathan. Although she had brought her lunch from home that day, she said she would. At lunchtime, they came back to the office. They were expecting to quickly eat the lunch Chelsea had ordered and then head to their next job. But, they found Chelsea talking on her phone and looking out the window. As soon as she saw them, she hung up the phone and greeted them with a smile. They found no lunch and it was obvious that Chelsea hadn't ordered lunch, nor had she cleaned, emptied the trash containers, or finished the filing.

Uncle Steve looked at the office and then calmly said, "Chelsea, I would've liked for you to work here for a long time, but I may have to let you go and get someone else."

Chelsea's eyes widened and turned red, and a tear started to run down her face. "But I didn't do anything wrong," she said very timidly.

"Right now," Uncle Steve explained in a soft voice, "I'm not concerned with something you did wrong, but with the things you failed to do right. When you decided not to do your best work you decided that the company didn't matter; only what you wanted to do mattered. When you didn't order lunch, you decided that Jonathan and I didn't need to eat and that we didn't matter. If you had thrown our lunch away, we would be hungry. If you don't order our lunch, we are hungry. Either way, we don't get to eat. Do you understand?"

Chelsea nodded while wiping her tears and reached in her handbag for her own lunch that she had brought with her. She offered it to Uncle Steve, but he refused and gave her a fatherly hug. "No, we'll go get some lunch, and I want you to go with us. Okay?" Chelsea nodded again, and he continued, "Now, turn the CLOSED sign around and let's go eat."

The memory faded and Jonathan's thoughts returned to the classroom.

He picked up his coffee cup and found it hot and full. "I'm beginning to see that not only have I done some things wrong, but I have failed to do the right thing even more often. I definitely need to change and let people see me doing more things right than wrong. I think that's been my problem. My friends see me doing more things they like, so I make them happier. Mom and the police see more things I do wrong, or don't do right, and I make them mad. I think that's my problem."

"Part of your problem is that you're falling into a trap. You don't understand the CIRCLE-F Principle. We can talk about that while we eat. Let me buy you lunch." Jonathan agreed. Angie declined their invitation to join them, so Jimmy and Jonathan drove off to Aunt Jo's.

Chapter 5

CIRCLE-F; Temptation

The diner parking lot always seemed to have more cars than it had parking spaces. No one admitted going to Aunt Jo's to talk; they went there to eat. But everyone talked more than they ate, and everyone ate more than they should. Jimmy liked to arrive just after the main lunch crowd because he could sometimes find a parking place then. That strategy worked for him today. A red-haired man backed out of a space near the door just as Jimmy pulled into the parking lot. Jonathan recognized him from somewhere, but something else caught his eye before he could remember where.

A small group of people huddled near a picnic table were motioning for Jonathan to join them. Jonathan's friends, some of whom had just been texting him this morning, called out to him. Jimmy nodded slightly and went ahead to get a table while Jonathan went to talk to them. Jonathan's stomach churned as he approached the group. He considered them to be his friends, but their relationship had been strained since the incident with Katie and his arrest. His presence completed the regular party group he hung out with for the last couple of years. Since his latest jail excursion, they hadn't all been together until now.

Although they had been his friends he couldn't help but notice they looked more like accusers than friends today. He could see why Katie sometimes said she felt uncomfortable with them. Without thinking, he reached up and stretched the collar of his shirt. As he inhaled he thought he detected the slight smell of beer, but that might just be his imagination. After all, most of his other memories with this group actually did include that smell.

They would've told you they were free spirited, but the truth is that the group reeked of rebellion. Most of the things they did carried the hidden intent of going against what they knew to be right. They all had the immature idea that being an adult meant rebelling against what their parents or teachers would consider the "right things." Being bad had become a badge of honor within their pack.

Eight people waited for Jonathan as he walked across the parking lot. He, Katie, and this group had been together for many weekend parties, and embarrassments, in the last couple of months.

Hannah was nineteen with long blonde hair. Her parents were upstanding leaders in the community and she resented the expectations that seemed to put on her. From her early teen years, she had decided to show her peers that she didn't have to be good. In her zeal to show her independence, she had fallen into the trap of rebellion. She sought the acceptance of her peers no matter what the costs, and all of her social media posts showed it. If this group thought it was the cool thing to do, she did, too. Reputation and group acceptance outweighed everything else.

Omar could easily claim to be the leader of the pack. His age and street knowledge gave him a head start on the party life that they all followed. His father had never been part of his life, and his mother had worked two jobs just to keep their apartment. This meant that he had been on the streets with some of the other kids from the projects from an early age.

Pete, Elle, and Sha'qui shared ethnic background with Omar, and very similar life experiences. Elle was the only one who had grown up in a two-parent home. She had been in church until just before she turned seventeen, when she had fallen to the lure of the street and the charm of Omar. She had said she'd do almost anything for Omar, and he believed it. Over the past four years, she had become more of a partier and less of a family member. Jonathan couldn't remember her talking about her last church visit.

Although they weren't dating, Pete and Sha'qui always seemed to sit close to one another. Pete's grandmother had left him her house in her will, and no one else in their group owned property.

Lexi showed an overwhelming desire to be accepted, but still seemed to Jonathan to have some internal compass that kept her from drifting too far. At twenty-one, she had a good job and a promising career; if the parties didn't interfere. She seemed to have been part of the group from a sense of convenience and companionship more than anything. Jonathan knew she had never had a stable family life and she often said she thought of the group as her family.

Samson and Edgar just lived for right now and whatever felt good. Either one would be willing to leave work early and get drunk. Both had carried illegal substances to work in their lunch boxes on more than one occasion and as recently as last week.

As Jonathan got close to the table, his dry mouth and rapid heartbeat added to the awkwardness of the moment. For the first time he wondered if any of them spent the night in jail the same night he did. They had all been together earlier in the evening, but after a certain number of drinks the night got too fuzzy for him to remember.

He saw Hannah, Lexi, Elle, and Sha'qui huddled on one end of the table. They were whispering. Smoldering cigarette butts in a container on the table told him at least two of them had been smoking. The spiral-bound notebook that they used to plan parties lay open on the table next to them. Omar, Edgar, Pete, and Samson were standing together and facing Jonathan.

"See, Brothers, I told you he wasn't dead," Omar teased. "Man, where have you been?"

Edgar continued prodding Jonathan while pretending he was giving confidential information. "You need to come on back to the party world before you forget how!"

"Yeah," Elle and Sha'qui said almost at the same time.

"You don't have to have Katie with you to party with us. Never did before!" Sha'qui finished the jab. They all knew what had happened and that Katie and Jonathan were no longer together.

Jonathan could clearly hear the bitterness and sharpness of each invitation. He could see the expectation in their eyes. They fully expected him to buckle under the pressure and ask about the next party. In just a few seconds, he sized up the group and decided on his answer. He looked at each one and mentally viewed their biographies before he answered.

Hannah, Omar, Pete, Elle, Lexi, Edgar, Samson, and Sha'qui. Individually he still cared for each of them. He held no anger or resentment toward them for anything. But, together this group represented the lifestyle that Jonathan had vowed to leave. For his own future, for his own integrity, he had to say good-bye to the lifestyle. That meant saying good-bye to the group and what it represented.

"We've had a lot of fun together," Jonathan started, "but I have to make some changes. I guess I just can't do it anymore. I'm sorry, and I don't mean to hurt you, but…"

"Man, you're just dreaming!" Omar interrupted. "You know you can never change!"

"You must think you're better than us now," Pete accused and Edgar and Samson agreed.

Sha'qui turned to Elle and Hannah, "He'll be back; you can bet on that! It's in his blood."

With wide eyes and an open mouth, Lexi watched and listened. She started to say something, but she seemed to have no words to fit her feelings. She had always talked about how they would still be together when they were old and would still be partying just as they did now. If Jonathan left now it would mean this couldn't be a forever kind of lifestyle for all of them.

A confused Jonathan turned and walked toward the diner door. The scoffing and accusing voices chased deaf ears and numbed senses. He no longer felt hungry or thirsty. In fact, for a moment he didn't feel anything. Walking away from these friends left such a hole in him. Losing Katie had left such a hole in him. Then he suddenly began to feel something. He felt empty and alone.

Walking into Aunt Jo's changes a person's world. Literally. From the sidewalk to the dining room, the lighting changes, the smells get richer, the temperature changes, voices replace car noises, and even floor texture gets smoother. All of a person's senses are stimulated in a different way immediately. The changes are not just physical. Even travelers talk about the immediate feeling of family. Today, Jonathan noticed the family atmosphere more than usual. His shoulders began to relax. He thought he might be able to eat something after all.

Jimmy sat with his back to the corner at a small square table at the far end of the dining room. He waved when he saw Jonathan. He already had a glass of tea in front of him and another appeared to be waiting for Jonathan. Crossing the dining room reminded Jonathan of playing football, but in slow motion. He dodged tables and people's heads and hands as they gestured and talked. After a small distraction, he almost bumped into Joy as she was pouring tea for someone. Joy danced around him, though, and never spilled a drop. She had been doing this for a long time. She just kept smiling and pouring.

Jonathan sat in the chair on Jimmy's left so they could both see the room. Their food arrived almost as soon as Jonathan sat down.

"I hope you don't mind that I went ahead and ordered for you," Jimmy said.

Jonathan laughed. "They don't have anything bad on the menu. I like it all!" He reached for his fork and Jimmy continued.

"Do you mind if I pray before we eat?"

Jonathan had nothing against prayer, but never thought about praying before his meals. "Not at all," he answered.

"Great and loving God, thank you for the provision of food. Would you please bless it so that it nourishes and strengthens our bodies? And would you please give Jonathan wisdom and comfort as he explores changes in his life? Thank you for answering our prayer of faith that we have humbly asked in Jesus' name. Amen." The short prayer sounded more like a short conversation with an old friend than the prayers Jonathan had heard at church gatherings.

When he finished, Jimmy started to eat. The restaurant buzzed with conversation and some occasional laughter. Jonathan took the silence at their table as an invitation to talk. He had never felt as trapped as he did now, and he hoped Jimmy could help.

"I really do need wisdom. It's hard to make life changes when you're not sure what's really right for you. It's so hard to make my friends happy and make my mom happy when their expectations are so different. I tried hanging out with my friends and not letting Mom know. I figured that what she didn't know wouldn't hurt her. Then I got myself arrested again. I couldn't stand the look in her eyes. I vowed never to do that to her again. So I just told my friends I couldn't party with them anymore. They all told me that I couldn't change. I feel like I'm trapped."

For a few moments they ate in silence. Jimmy finished his meal and let Joy take his plate when she came by and left the check. Most of the other customers started to leave and the room gradually grew less noisy as Jonathan finished his meal. Jimmy placed some cash on top of the check while wiping off the table in front of him. Joy came by, picked up the cash and looked at Jimmy for a second.

"I won't need any change today, Joy, that's all for you. Thanks. The food was great, as always," he said, and started to turn back toward Jonathan.

Joy didn't leave, so he paused and looked at her again. Jonathan thought he looked slightly puzzled. Joy was smiling and reaching into her pocket.

"Do you need a pen, Jimmy?" she asked playfully as she offered him hers.

Jimmy paused for just a brief moment, began to smile, and said, "Please."

Only after she left did Jonathan realize that Jimmy had spread a napkin in front of him as if he planned to write on it. He had been checking his pockets just before Joy walked up. Jonathan smiled to himself. Writing on napkins must be something Jimmy did regularly. Joy had seen him checking his pockets and knew he was looking for a pen.

Jimmy took the pen and drew a circle about the size of a quarter. Then he wrote an "F" in the middle with the bottom of the F touching the bottom of the circle.

"When we were at the office, I told you that you were falling into a trap. Just now, you said you felt 'trapped.' Understanding the CIRCLE-F Principle will help you avoid those traps."

"What is that?" Jonathan asked. He focused on Jimmy's words so intensely that he didn't hear anything else in the diner. He listened closely as Jimmy continued.

"CIRCLE-F is an acrostic for 'Confusing Integrity and Reputation Can Lead to Endangerment of your Future.' It means that you endanger your future if you confuse your personal integrity with your reputation. Remember, your integrity is who you really are, and *should be* good, whole, complete, solid, sound, and dependable. Your reputation is what you and others say or think about you. You can endanger your future in two ways. I call them traps. You faced the first trap when you tried to hide the breaches in your integrity from your mother. You also tried to hide them from y-"

"From myself," Jonathan interrupted. "I remember thinking and saying that what my mom didn't know wouldn't hurt her. But it hurt worse when she found out later. It also hurt Katie, and me, and ..." his voice trailed off as he felt the hurts again.

"That's right," Jimmy agreed in a kind tone as he put his hand on Jonathan's shoulder. "That is your living example of the childish notion that 'it's not wrong if you don't get caught.' If you think about your life in terms of our coffee cup examples, you thought that turning the leak so that you couldn't see it would keep it from leaking. Many famous people have made the same mistake."

Jonathan thought for a second and said, "Yeah, I can name you some in the news in the last few weeks."

"Exactly. As long as everyone else thought they were okay, they were willing to pretend they were okay. They fell into the first trap: a hidden breach is not a breach, so, if people say I'm okay I must be okay."

"Yeah," Jonathan nodded, "and I was in that trap with them."

"The real truth is that what we do generally flows out of who we are. So, any breach in behavior shows a breach in personal integrity. You know, like coffee running on the table shows a leak in the cup."

Jonathan perked up. "So what if I want to fix the cup before I put coffee in it? What if I want to fix *me* before I do something wrong?"

"Then you're working on your personal integrity already! The want-to is the first step." Jimmy's voice showed his excitement. "Now don't step in the second trap."

Jonathan leaned back slightly and snapped his fingers. "I was just about to ask about the second trap."

"It was laid out in front of you in the parking lot. Didn't your friends tell you that you couldn't change?"

Jonathan's slow nod indicated that he understood and was working to process the information. He, himself, had begun to wonder if he could change and that made him feel empty and hopeless.

"Well, that's a reputation statement. You do have the potential to change, and you can do it. If you buy the lie that you cannot change, you won't. You *will* make your reputation a devastating reality. You're working on changing from the inside out. Don't let discouragement from outside sources get inside."

As clearly as Jonathan could see the CIRCLE-F drawing on the napkin he could also see how he had fallen. Not knowing that one principle had allowed him to fall into both of the traps. For a moment he felt embarrassed and frustrated. He had believed that hiding his breaches meant they would have no consequences. More than once he had bought the lie that he couldn't change. He felt his anger rise. For a moment he directed it at Jimmy, then he realized Jimmy only wanted to help him.

All right, he said to himself, *I committed to change, and he is trying to help me. I've got to learn to listen better.* He inhaled and looked from the napkin to Jimmy's eyes.

"Okay, Jimmy, I want to change. Would I be right in assuming you can help me with a plan?"

Jimmy smiled and patted Jonathan on the shoulder as he stood. "We'll start talking about building a foundation for your integrity next week." Jimmy said. He handed Jonathan the napkin. "You keep this."

Just as they reached for the door handle to leave, Joy called out, "Have a nice afternoon!"

Jonathan thought for certain he had seen her wink at Jimmy. He thought to himself, *I bet I'm not the first person to take home one of these napkins.*

Chapter 6

Starting to Build

For the next few days, Jonathan worked almost twelve hours a day with Uncle Steve. For many of those days, he worked digging the footers for three houses and a new store. Digging footers simply meant that he'd dig a hole or trench to hold concrete for the foundation. Every building needs a different type or size of footer. The key is to make the footer deep and wide enough to hold all the weight of the building when it's finished. After the surveyors decide where the building is going to sit, the footer is actually the starting point of the building.

Jonathan usually didn't get to watch much of the building construction process after he finished the footers and waterlines. When the waterlines, septic tanks, and footers were finished, he usually moved to the next job. This week, he worked on two houses that were side by side. When he finished the second house and loaded to leave, he talked to the block masons who were working on the first house. He always marveled at the speed with which they laid the blocks for walls. They seemed so fast. Today, his curiosity made him ask about the care they seemed to be taking with the first one.

The 5'8" block mason introduced himself as Ralph Norman. "I am sixty, but I have been here since I was seventeen. I moved here from Michigan," he said with a smile. Jonathan could tell that he still had some of his Michigan accent. When Jonathan expressed surprise at the amount of time Ralph spent on the first block, he found out how much Ralph liked to talk.

"That block is called a cornerstone. You have to start constructing a block building on the corner. You have to make sure that the building is square and level. The four cornerstones of a building are the most important building blocks in the whole structure. The only thing more important is the foundation. If the building isn't square, it will be very hard to put the walls up. It will be almost impossible to do the floors inside and the roof on top." He tapped on the first cornerstone he had laid, "That one block – old masons called it the 'chief cornerstone' – is the most important."

"I can see that," Jonathan agreed. "If you put that one block in the wrong place or at the wrong angle, it affects the whole building." He thought for a minute while Ralph started placing other blocks. "Is that where the concept of calling a ball player the 'cornerstone' of the team came from?"

"That's right!" Ralph beamed. "They call them that when the team strategy is built around that one player."

When Ralph got distracted with his crew, Jonathan took the opportunity to slip away to his truck. He had no idea how many times he had seen Ralph on jobs before. He wondered now why he had never stopped and talked to him before. He made a mental note to speak to Ralph when he saw him on a worksite again. He had found Ralph interesting and easy to talk to.

The napkin with the CIRCLE-F drawing on it was still in Jonathan's truck. He looked at it every day as a reminder. Jonathan found his new life challenging and comforting at the same time. He really missed his old friends and the fun times. He didn't miss those rough mornings of having to explain to Uncle Steve why he needed to be late or wouldn't be in to work at all. Still, he felt empty sometimes in the evenings when he ate his dinner alone and watched whatever was on television. Sometimes he'd read, but always he missed the social interaction with his friends. And he REALLY missed Katie. At least, he missed having someone like Katie.

Looking back on their time together, Jonathan didn't know if he could really say that he was in love with Katie. Maybe he had loved her on some level, but he didn't know how deeply. He did love the idea of having someone to talk to and spend special time with, especially at night. *I must be crazy*, he thought. *I'm lonely but I don't want to be with the friends I had.*

I want a special person to spend my evenings with, but I don't know who. He decided he really needed to talk to Jimmy again. The reminder he'd left for himself on his phone said they were to meet the next morning.

Jimmy's office smelled like coffee and Jonathan was pleased to find Angie had already poured him a cup. Jimmy had his coffee and smiled when he came in the room.

"Looks like you have been working hard on those new houses. I drove by and saw you working and talking to Ralph yesterday."

Jonathan smiled. It always makes a man feel good inside when another man acknowledges that he has been working hard. "Yes, sir! And it's so dusty that it takes me almost as long to clean up as I spend working."

They both laughed. Then, Jonathan told Jimmy and Angie about the new construction and the workload he had. New construction is good for the local economy, so everyone is interested. He talked about the jobs and the locations as they made themselves comfortable in the chairs in the conference room. After several minutes of conversation, Jonathan started talking about making extra money and saving some.

"All the extra work means I have a little more money to set aside," he said. "I am saving for when I get married." His voice trailed off as he suddenly thought about Katie and how lonely his evenings were without her. Sometimes his home seemed so empty and he felt so alone. He crossed his legs and began staring at his boots. Angie refilled their coffee and excused herself. Jonathan got very quiet as the thoughts and feelings filled his mind. He wiggled his mouth and nose as if he had an itch and softly said, "Sometimes I sure feel lonely and lost."

"Starting a new life like you're trying to do is very hard," Jimmy said as he leaned toward Jonathan. "Changing friends and interests is never easy."

Jonathan exhaled loudly and shook his head. "When I had that encounter with my friends at the diner, I was very hurt at first. Then, after you and I talked, I felt really good. During these last few days, I've talked to some of them. They made it clear that we can't be friends unless I drink and do drugs with them. This week I've been lonely and am wondering if I'm making the right decisions. Is there a way to really know? I mean, you know, without having to wait five years and look back?"

"I have two answers for you," Jimmy began. "First, no one can truly know everything, so no, you can't always know ahead of time whether the decision is the right one. But, most of the time you can make good decisions by looking five years ahead."

"Ahead?" Jonathan's head snapped around to face Jimmy and his eyes widened. "You mean look into the future?"

"Yes." The answer sounded simple and blunt.

Before Jonathan asked another question he pondered the answer. "But how," Jonathan spoke slowly as he tried to understand, "can I predict the future?"

"I'm not talking about predicting someone's future, Jonathan, I'm talking about building your own. Think about this: if you wanted to go to jail next week, could you make that happen?"

"I think I can pretty well say I know how to go to jail!" Jonathan laughed.

"Well, if you don't want to go to jail next week, do you know how to stay out? Listen, I'm not just talking about jail. This isn't a short term question. I'm asking you if you have a life plan. Do you know what is important to you, and do you have a plan to get there?"

"Honestly, no. I've just let life happen. Sometimes I have a plan for next week, but not five years from now. I never really thought about it. How do you do that?"

"There are a lot of steps if you want to do it right. Every journey begins with knowing who you are and where you are. Then, you decide where you want to go. So, you start by deciding what kind of person you want to be. Then work on where you're going and what you want to do."

Jonathan remembered playing in his back yard as a child. The neighbors saw a little boy running around swinging a stick. In his mind he saw himself riding a war horse, wearing armor, and swinging a huge sword as he fought dragons and evildoers. He smiled to himself and said softly, "I remember, as a child, wanting to be a prince and rescue the damsel in distress. I had my own castle and everything. I played that game almost every day."

"I think that's almost a universal dream. Think about it, how many times have you heard the statement, 'A man's home is his castle'? Most little boys will pick up a stick or toy sword and pretend to be fighting the enemy. My niece would rather dress up like a princess than anything else. Everyone seems to be fascinated by knights, castles, and moats."

"Yeah," Jonathan leaned forward and rested his elbows on his knees. He bowed his head and his voice faded. "Then you grow up and find out that the whole thing is just a dream. I thought I would be Katie's prince. I thought we had part of our future planned out. Then I destroyed everything in our relationship in one night. I went from hero to zero to minus one princess in about four hours." He grunted. "Kingdom lost."

"More accurately, castle crumbled." Jimmy waited for Jonathan to respond.

Almost a minute passed before Jonathan looked up and said, "What's the difference? Either way I lost her and destroyed all that I thought I'd been working for…What we'd been planning for."

"Jonathan, I don't know what happened that night. What I've gathered from what you've told me is that you had a breach. You had such a breach in your character that the spillover in behavior hurt Katie. In fact, it hurt her so much that she left you. It appears to me that your castle of character has crumbled and you have nothing left for kingdom building. Am I right?"

"Yes, but how do I rebuild it?" Jonathan asked.

"You start with the foundation," Jimmy pointed at Jonathan's muddy boots, "like you've been doing with the houses this week. You build your personal integrity from the foundation upward, just like you'd build a building."

The memory of Ms. Brown's office and the first day with Jimmy flashed on Jonathan's mind. "That makes Ms. Brown's statement about getting my house in order even clearer, in a way. But what foundation are you talking about? If my integrity is about who I am, do I build my castle of character on me?"

"In a way, yes." Jimmy started. "The foundation for your integrity is your personal core values. That's not an abstract set of ideas, but a concrete way of thinking about what's really important to you. People usually think of values as abstract things like loyalty or commitment. The core values I'm talking about are the things that are valuable to you at the core of your existence – your heart values or your true loves. Core values are everything in your life that is as important to you as you are, or more. Let's talk about your core values for a few minutes. Name something that you think might be a core value to you."

"Well, judging by what you just said about me being part of the foundation, and a core value being everything in my life as important to me as I am or more, I would say *I* am one of my core values."

Jimmy nodded and smiled. "Good! Some people need more prompting to start looking at themselves in that way. *You* are the starting point of your core values. What is another one?"

"I would have to say my family, especially my mother." Jonathan immediately replied.

"Now think it through with me," Jimmy continued the teaching point. "Does your mother really meet the definition of a core value? Is she as important to you as you are, or more?"

Jonathan inhaled to answer, but hesitated. Then, very slowly he began, "Yyeess, because I really enjoyed the party life, but decided to stop partying mostly because of what I saw it doing to her. She didn't exactly push me to stop. But…" His eyes wandered around the room and he worked his mouth as if trying to form words he couldn't find. Finally, his eyes gleamed and he continued, "I decided on my own to stop because I love her and didn't like the pain that my partying was causing her."

"So she's more important to you than partying is?" Jimmy asked.

"I love her more than partying, so I quit partying to stop hurting her." After he said it, the full meaning of the words registered with Jonathan. His eyes welled up with tears.

Jimmy pretended not to notice the tears and asked Jonathan, "Do you have any more core values?"

"Yeah, my job."

"Why is your job important to you?"

Jonathan looked at Jimmy with wide eyes and a short gasp. Until Jimmy said that, he thought he had this core values thing figured out completely. "I need money, and my job is how I get money."

Jimmy's questions continued, "Why do you need money?"

"Because I have to pay my bills or I will lose my apartment and I won't be able to eat!"

"And why do you need an apartment? Why do you need to eat?" Jimmy wouldn't stop the questions.

"Because I…" Jonathan stopped abruptly. He suddenly realized where the questions were leading. "Because I am a core value." Then he chuckled, "Because I love me!"

"That makes sense. Your job is a tool you're using to provide for yourself. You are the core value that makes you want to work. So you love you, and you love your mother and family. Are those your only core values?"

"Is it bad that I can't say my whole family is a core value?" Jonathan asked. "Many of my family are so caught up in alcohol and drugs that we can't have much of a relationship. I do love them, but, well, you know."

"I do understand. Although the circumstances are different, everyone would have to say the same thing. I have some distant cousins that I don't even know."

Jonathan absent-mindedly reached for the coffee cup and found it full and hot. He noticed Jimmy sipping from his cup. Jonathan thought back on his visits since he met Angie. His coffee cup never seemed to be empty. He had noticed it before, but now his curiosity made him ask, "Why does Angie take such care to fill our coffee cups? She's your employee, but I get the feeling that it's not something you told her to do. Even if you did tell her to fill yours, why would she bother with mine?"

Jimmy looked at him and smiled. "The simple answer is that she just does it because she is Angie. This is the perfect time for you to ask that question, though. One of Angie's core values is her family. Since her family is important, the family atmosphere is important. Since her family is important to her, and since we're someone's family, we must be important, too. The behavior of expressing the value of family flows naturally out of Angie because of the heart value of her own family. Does that make sense?"

Jonathan thought for a moment, and said, "I think so." All of this seemed like such a deep concept to him. He honestly didn't know if he did fully understand.

"Maybe if I put it on a more personal level, you will understand. Angie has had family who needed to know the kinds of things we teach here. Since she loves her family, and since everyone who comes in here is *someone's* family, she wants them to feel comfortable. She treats everyone like family. Because of her core value of her family, she cares for other people's families. She knows you have value and she chooses to show that you have value because of how much she loves her own family. Does that make sense?"

"Yeah. She doesn't just think 'do unto others as you would have them do unto you'; she thinks 'do unto others' families as you want others to do unto your family'."

"Right."

"I really do understand," Jonathan replied. "Because I have been thinking this week that I wanted to do a good job on the footers for these houses because someone like me will have his family there. I would want mine done right, so I'm going to do his right. Since I know I'm important, I know that whoever lives there is important, too."

Jimmy nodded and smiled as he said, "That is part of the cornerstone of respect, based on the core value of you. We will talk about that later, but you're really on the right track. Let's get back to talking about your core values. Other than you and your mother, what other core values do you have?"

"Until recently, I would've added some of my friends, but I've found out that they are not really friends after all. Since I'm changing close friend groups, I don't really have any. Can friends ever really be that close?"

"Absolutely!" Jimmy responded so firmly that it surprised Jonathan. "I should clarify that, though. Only friends who are so close that you would consider them family would be in that category. Not everyone you would call a friend would necessarily be a core value. One of my close friends is David Self."

A flash of recognition crossed Jonathan's face. "Isn't he the one they call Reverend at that coffee house on the corner near the building supply store?" Jimmy nodded so Jonathan continued. "He's a great guy. I see him there sometimes when I go in and get a waffle in the morning."

"That's the one," Jimmy said. "Some of them call him Preacher. He wrote a book about the ministry he does there called <u>Everything I Know about Evangelism I Learned at a Coffee House</u>. He wrote it about his experiences there. He comes by here a couple of times a week and we have coffee and talk."

"Does he come to see you or to get some of Angie's coffee?" Jonathan teased.

"Well, he always gets coffee first," Jimmy admitted as he laughed. Then he looked thoughtfully at Jonathan. "For you, changing friends may mean that you don't have any that you would consider close enough to be core values. That may be different in a few months as you develop new relationships. Do you have any more core values?"

"I'm not trying to shift the conversation, but I have to honestly say that I'm having kind of a hard time thinking about people as values. Every time you say 'core values' I have to adjust my thinking in order to answer. Like you said earlier, I think of values as concepts." Jonathan looked almost afraid as he waited for Jimmy's answer. He really didn't want to offend Jimmy, but he wanted to be honest. The basic information did seem to be helping him some, but the new way of saying it challenged him.

"I understand fully. Sometimes I wonder if there is a better way to say it. I'll explain in a little while why I don't say it another way, if that's okay." Jimmy didn't seem offended at all.

"Sure, that's fine. I guess, since we were talking about the Reverend, I should list church or something." Jonathan figured that would be something Jimmy would expect.

"Why?"

That question caught Jonathan off guard completely. He had expected a pat on the back or some affirmation for the mention of church. He hadn't expected a challenge. When he inhaled to answer, he caught himself. *Because that's what I thought you expected me to say* is probably not a good answer, he decided. Jonathan's mental confusion caused him to take so long to answer that Jimmy asked him again, this time with more focus.

"Why would you want to list church as a core value? Is church that important to you? Do you have a church home?"

Jimmy's simple questions hit Jonathan like ocean waves. He had never thought about church and home as similar concepts. The thought of feeling at home in a church building had never crossed his mind. He did think that church could be important. He could remember some of his family telling him he needed to go to church. But was church really that important to him? He almost never attended and really didn't enjoy it when he did. Jonathan suddenly became aware of the very loud silence in the room as Jimmy awaited his answers.

"Is it bad if I don't know?" Jonathan's humble tone showed some of the despair he felt.

"It's good that you admit it." The soft and comforting voice of Jimmy almost seemed to reach inside Jonathan and ease some of the pain he felt.

"Listen, deciding what your core values are is the single most important thing you will ever do in your life. You have to decide for yourself what's important. Your core values will form the basis on which you make all your conscious decisions. My questions were to help you decide for yourself what your core values are. When you said you should 'list church or something', it was almost the same thing as saying 'I love my mother or somebody'. It didn't show a core value level commitment. Is this making sense?"

It truly did make sense to Jonathan. Scary sense. He considered himself an adult, a full-grown man. Yet he couldn't answer a simple question about what or who was really important to him. No wonder everything seemed to be so out of control in his life. He felt a sudden rush of goosebumps run up his back and a sick feeling in the pit of his stomach. The realization loomed in front of him as ugly as a monster from a horror movie. Until recently, the important things in his life had been his own personal pleasure, sexual arousal, and the high he got from alcohol or drugs. He had no clear foundation and no life plan.

"You're right, Jimmy. This is a hard process."

"I didn't say it was hard," Jimmy answered. "I said it was important. For many people it's a process, and you're right; it can be hard. You have to decide for yourself what your core values are, and you have to be sure of each one. No one can decide for you what your core values are. That's why I'm asking you so many questions. I'm not looking for certain answers. I don't have a preset list I'm trying to get you to find. I'm trying to help you find your own true core values."

Jonathan confessed, "I am starting to see that one of my problems has been that my only core value was partying. It was what I lived for, saved my money for, looked forward to all week, and built all of my plans around. I worked to make money so I could spend it on partying. Everything revolved around that."

"Don't let me put words in your mouth," started Jimmy, "but it sounds like an addiction. For building your personal integrity, your core values are everything in your life worth as much to you as you are, or more. The truth is that a good core value will lead to integrity. If the core value doesn't lead to integrity, you should consider it an addiction. Any behavior that you repeat until it begins to replace or destroy one or more of your core values is an addiction."

"I can see that," agreed Jonathan. "Like my craving for alcohol replaced my desire to be close with my mom. I was more interested in the parties than I was in the fact that it was hurting her. And costing her bail money, which I still need to pay back." He paused briefly, and continued, "Then I shook the beer bottle in Katie's face and screamed at her. I told her she was crazy if she thought she could mean more to me than a good drink. I don't drink every day, so I never thought I had an alcohol problem. Whether the alcohol or the partying, I'm starting to see that I might have an addiction. Even though I don't drink every day, alcohol still interferes with my relationships."

Jonathan's whole perception of himself changed. He felt sad and ashamed. He was surprised that he had gotten on this road in the first place. He regretted what he had done, and who he had become. He realized he had taken a wrong turn, but he decided that it didn't have to be the end of his life. It could be a new beginning. He just needed to figure out how to turn around.

While Angie silently refilled their coffee cups and Jonathan examined himself, Jimmy continued. "That's a good observation." Jimmy's voice had an encouraging tone. He pointed at Jonathan, smiled and continued, "You might want to go to an AA meeting or a Celebrate Recovery group. You can go and not participate. You can just watch and listen. You might learn something about yourself. Look, I'm not saying you're a drunk or an alcoholic. However, you just admitted that you might have an addiction, and those programs can help. You can also help yourself by changing your behavior."

"I can see where stopping that lifestyle will help my relationship with my mom. I'm pretty sure my relationship with Katie is finished. She's moved out of state with her family. Are you saying that just stopping my party habit will fix my other relationships?"

"No." Jimmy's voice had a reassuring tone. "You must work on your relationships like you were working on your party lifestyle. You repeated that behavior until it began to replace your core values. Now you have to repeat different behaviors to get a different result. You must repeat behaviors that become an application or fortification of your core values. That means that you're strengthening your commitment to those core values. Let me give you an example. I make it a point to ask my wife out on a date every week. We have a set night for our dates, but I always ask her to go out with me. That strengthens our bond. I grow to love her more because I practice loving her more. Then I'm more careful not to make decisions that would hurt her or reflect badly on her because I'm making decisions that make her feel treasured."

Jonathan had slid to the front of his chair, shifted his weight, and leaned forward. He felt, for the first time in years, as if someone really had good solid answers that made sense. In the last few days, and especially in the last few minutes, his life seemed to be coming into focus. It really was all about personal integrity all along. His breaches cost him the things he wanted most because he forgot that he wanted them most. More than partying or his so-called friends. What were his core values, his heart values, and his main loves?

"Okay," Jonathan eagerly began, "If my core values are the foundation for my lifestyle and I want to have a very successful life," he began to smile, "if I want to live the BIG life, are two core values enough? When we dig the foundation for a big house or store, we dig a big foundation. If I really want to live large, it seems like having my mom and myself for core values is too small. Those sound like little boy core values, not grown man core values. I would like to have a family one day, and a more solid friend group. I might want to get involved in church." He smiled and his eyes had a sparkle. "It's my turn to ask you. Does this make sense?"

"Oh, yeah!" Jimmy laughed. "That makes a lot of sense. I can see that you're beginning to understand. If you want friends, you must be a friend. If you want a relationship with God, you must be a friend of God." Jimmy decided that Jonathan's puzzled look meant he needed more explanation. "When you meet people, you learn their names. You might look at social media pages or go to social gatherings or hangouts. Then, you get to know something about their personalities, their likes and dislikes. If you have something in common, you might develop some level of relationship. After a while, you might become friends. You might even invite them to your home."

"That could take a while!" Jonathan interrupted. "I would need some time to clean up before that." He and Jimmy laughed. Jonathan's tone became serious and he continued. "I see what you mean. And if you hang out at the same places, you learn about one another quicker. I need to change the kinds of places I hang out at."

"Probably. And I'm not trying to preach at you or turn the conversation to religion, but you mentioned church. If you want a relationship with God, the process is the same. You learn His name, and find out about Him. To find out more about God, you read the Bible, attend churches and Bible studies, and spend time with other people who know Him. It's simple if you think about it. It's a cool thought, too. The God of the universe wants to know us."

"Wow!" Jonathan responded without thinking. "Yeah, it makes you think. It kind of gives me a sense of value. You know, it makes me feel like I'm important, in a way."

"It should. You should respect yourself and treat yourself as if you have value. We're going to be talking about that more in the days to come. I hate to cut us off, but I have a date with my wife. Let's get together again soon. Keep thinking about your core values and we'll talk about that some more, too. Feel free to call if you have any questions."

"I will," Jonathan said as he shook Jimmy's hand. "Thank you. I'll see you next week." Jonathan shook his hand and left.

From his truck, Jonathan watched Jimmy turn off the lights and make his way from the front door to his car. As Jonathan started his truck, he suddenly remembered the two cups of coffee they had left on the table to grow cold in the dark.

Chapter 7

The Distraction

Even while he and Jimmy talked, Jonathan had been planning his evening. Working on his core values and making a list of things he needed to do this week just seemed logical. He decided he would put a load of clothes in the washing machine and listen to music while he made the list. In a dream world, Jonathan would have his core values and his life worked out before bedtime. He'd focus on good core values and it would be easy to make decisions. In the real world, things just don't work that way. Distractions and disappointments seem to come in never ending waves. One quick phone call had his mind focused miles away.

Jonathan called his mother to tell her that he loved her and to offer to take her out to eat soon. When she answered the phone, her urgent words seemed to open a time capsule.

"I had just reached for my phone to call you!" his mother said, sounding almost alarmed. "Ashleigh Cole is here. She had just asked me if I could get in touch with you. We're at my house. Can you come now? We'll explain when you get here."

Ashleigh Cole and Jonathan had been friends for years. They would always be friends. A couple of years ago they had dated for a short time. That relationship had centered more on a love for drugs than a love for one another. They stopped dating when the police arrested Jonathan for disorderly conduct. Alcohol and anger really do not mix well. His probation wouldn't allow for drugs or alcohol usage, and he had to report weekly. Since his probation officer could test him at any time for drugs or alcohol, he temporarily stopped using both.

While Jonathan served his probation time, Ashleigh moved in with a guy named Robert. Jonathan had been angry at first, but he got over it quickly. Robert wasn't on probation, so he had no probation limits like Jonathan did. He did have enough money for drugs, which was what Ashleigh really wanted anyway. Jonathan understood, and moved on with his life. After all, who wants to stop heavy partying just because your partner has to stop? Jonathan had heard that Robert had a bad temper, but he didn't know him well.

Ashleigh hadn't been part of Jonathan's life for a long time. In fact, he rarely thought about her. The conversation with his mother had brought Ashleigh to the front of his thoughts. Memories of the good times they shared flowed through his mind as he drove.

He remembered looking into her big, sparkling blue eyes when she challenged him to race. "Jonathan, I bet I can beat you to those trash cans," she had said, and then she started running. She had beaten him, and he could almost hear her laughing now.

She had loved to play softball and basketball, too. Jonathan remembered that she had more energy than almost anyone else on her team. She could really hit, too. Then, later she had started using drugs and stopped playing sports almost completely. As he parked his truck, Jonathan thought about how much they had both changed.

When Jonathan reached for his mother's doorknob, he thought he heard crying inside. Opening the door revealed the source of the sound. He saw Ashleigh resting her head on his mother's shoulder. She sobbed and shivered as she looked up at him. He looked into the eyes of a woman he did not know. The confident young woman who loved to race and play ball didn't look back at him. The Ashleigh he knew lived life to the fullest. She loved to party and she loved to run and laugh. She even liked to wrestle.

The woman who looked back at him now seemed to have no life in her bloodshot eyes. One eye looked like the eye of a woman ten years older than Ashleigh. The other eye, swollen and turning black, looked like it belonged to a professional fighter. Blood from her swollen lip and broken nose stained the towel and icepack she held. Dried blood on her shirt and pants and told him that this had happened much earlier in the day.

"Ash, what happened? Where is your car?" He assumed she had been in a car wreck. Even as he asked, he saw the clear imprint of a fist on her cheek. Someone had beaten her. *Has she been mugged or raped?* he thought to himself. Before he could think about how to word his question, she answered.

"It's really all my fault. Robert told me not to spend that much money on groceries. I didn't think ten dollars would matter. But he knows better than I do about how much we have to spend." She looked down at her trembling hands "I told him I was sorry, but…" She paused as she raised two fingers gently to her swollen eye.

Jonathan's already pounding heart sped up. His face turned red and he began to sweat. Every muscle in his body seemed ready to explode. His teeth clenched and both hands rolled into fists. The lights seemed to get brighter in the room as his pupils dilated. Each breath hissed through his teeth. He could hear his own heart beating. "Where. Is. He?" he growled.

"No, Jonathan," Ashleigh began, "I told you it's my fault. I made him mad. Don't say anything to him. Please!"

"I don't plan on doing a lot of talking," Jonathan stated flatly. "I plan to explain, man to man, how I feel." Both of his fists shook when he said it.

* * *

Samantha Timms knew her son well. She knew that Jonathan would go to prison if she let him leave the house now. No more county jail, no more chances; he would go to prison for killing Robert – or Robert would kill him. She understood his anger. She almost felt the same way. Still, she knew she couldn't let him leave the house. How could she stop him? She inhaled to say something when Ashleigh spoke.

"He's at home, at our house." Her quiet voice faded into sobs again.

Samantha watched her son storm out the door. She couldn't stop him now. Tears streamed down her face as she cried with Ashleigh. Two broken women faced cold truths in their lives, as the room grew dark in the twilight. Samantha helped Ashleigh clean up, and then treated her injuries the best she could. She offered to take her to the emergency room or to the Healthcare Afterhours office, but Ashleigh refused. Samantha focused all her mothering instincts on Ashleigh while trying not to think about losing her son to prison – or death. If only she could have stopped him from leaving!

* * *

Jonathan gripped the steering wheel in his truck. Every negative and violent emotion he'd had in the last few weeks now had an outlet. He no longer had to be angry at an event or set of circumstances. Now he could be angry with someone for a specific reason. Anger swelled up inside Jonathan until he thought he'd explode. While he drove he fantasized about hitting Robert. First he thought about using his fist, then about using a chair or piece of firewood, or something similar. Then he daydreamed about choking him.

While turning onto the street where Robert lived, Jonathan tried to decide whether he would hit Robert first or strangle him. His truck easily drove over the curb in front of the house and onto the grass. Jonathan jumped out and started for the front door, which hadn't been closed fully. He could hear a voice from inside the house that made him slow down before he jerked open the door. Maybe Robert had a surprise waiting for him.

Through the slightly open door, Jonathan could see only the back of a chair and the top of Robert's head. Cursing and occasionally stomping his foot in a drunken rage, Robert never heard Jonathan enter the room. Jonathan listened to him babble for a few minutes, getting angrier as he listened. He pieced together what had been happening from the mumbling and rambling. He couldn't hold himself back anymore when he clearly heard Robert say, "They won't lock me up. She deserved it. She said she wanted to get some food. I gave her some money for that. She knew that other money was my drinking money."

Robert seemed not to hear the door squeak or the floor creak. Jonathan stopped just behind him and to his left. He stepped forward two steps. Just over the arm of the chair, he could see the bottle in Robert's dirty hand. Another step. He could see the unshaven face and the wet shirt below it.

The strong smell of liquor and vomit didn't slow Jonathan down much. Anger drove him. He wanted Robert to see what was coming, so he wouldn't hit him from behind. He looked quickly around the room for something to hit Robert with, then gripped his fist.

Deliberately, Jonathan stepped around the chair where Robert could see him. Drunk or sober, Jonathan didn't care. Jonathan cared about Ashleigh, although he had never been in love with her. They had known one another for a long time and had been close friends. No woman, no person, deserved what Robert did to her. Every ounce of anger and bitterness Jonathan had ever had for anyone or anything waited for him to release it now. He tensed up and began to draw back to hit the drunken monster with his fist.

Robert looked up at Jonathan and straight into his eyes. Then, as if he had been talking to Jonathan all along, he said, "I told her she was crazy if she thought she could mean more to me than a good drink."

For the shortest of moments, Jonathan saw *himself* sitting in that chair. Without warning and without intending to, he threw up all over Robert. His eyes rolled back and he almost fainted. His knees buckled and he fell to the floor. The room seemed to be hot and cold at the same time. It seemed to spin and the floor suddenly felt uneven and unsteady.

Jonathan had said those exact words to Katie the night she left him. The exact words. With the same disrespectful attitude. The reality of who he had been and what he had done to Katie engulfed him. Jonathan crawled to the door and desperately made his way back to his truck.

He had seen himself as a valiant knight coming to Ashleigh's rescue. He had come here to kill an ogre. But instead of an ugly enemy or an ogre, he had found a real-life reflection of himself in that chair. Although he had never hit a woman with his fist as Robert had done, he had hit Katie, his mom, and maybe others with his words instead. He gagged again. His hands shook, sweat poured down his forehead and soaked through his shirt. Somehow, he had failed to see those closest to him as people with feelings. He hadn't seen hurt in their eyes. He came here thinking of himself as a conquering knight. He found himself leaving as the ogre's twin.

When he finally sat in the driver's seat of his truck, he didn't have the energy to put the key in the ignition. He sat in the darkness of the truck with an even deeper darkness in his heart. Helpless, hopeless, and in complete despair he wished he could just die right there. In all his life he had never hated anyone more than he hated himself right now. What if he did die? He would never be able to make up for all that he had done. He'd never be able to undo the hurt he had caused. He thought about the knife on his belt, the rope in the back of his truck. Death could come quite easily.

An explosion of light jarred him out of his private world of despair. A voice from beyond the light spoke in a loud, firm voice. "Mr. Timms, please put your hands on the steering wheel where I can see them." The voice belonged to one of the officers who had arrested him before. "Now, please!"

Jonathan's mind flashed back to the other times this had happened to him. Those times, drugs or alcohol had been involved. This time he had nothing in his system stronger than coffee. When he put his hands on the steering wheel, the officer slowly opened the door. "Do you have a weapon?" the officer asked before Jonathan could move.

"No, Sir, just my work knife," Jonathan responded quickly.

"Would you please step out of the vehicle?" the officer requested in a tone that said he wouldn't accept *no* for an answer. "I need to see your license and insurance card."

Jonathan still felt weak so he moved very slowly. He exited the truck and gave the officer his license. The officer began to explain, "Mr. Timms, the reason I'm detaining you is that we had a call describing your truck. The call said that your truck drove here quickly, jumped the curb, and then slid to a stop near the doorsteps. Have you been drinking?"

"No."

"Are you under the influence of any drugs or medications, prescription or otherwise?"

"No."

"Would you be willing to take a test to verify your answers?"

For the first time in his adult life, Jonathan could answer this one with a smile. "Sure!"

"Are you injured?"

"No."

"Mr. Timms, can you tell us how your truck wound up parked in Mr. Dale's front yard?" a woman's voice asked.

For the first time Jonathan noticed the second officer. He thought for a moment before he answered. He decided that *because I was mad and came to kill him* would be the kind of answer that wouldn't make the evening end well. He decided to go for absolute simplicity. "I was in a hurry to talk to him. I'm sorry."

One officer went to the front door while the other stayed near Jonathan and watched him. After tapping on the open door, the officer entered and almost immediately came back out. "He's obviously very intoxicated and has puked everywhere!" The officer reported. "I'm calling an ambulance." After a quick call to the dispatch officer, she returned. "He keeps talking to himself but he's too drunk for me to make out what he's saying."

Jonathan debated whether he should tell everything he knew or just answer their questions. He decided that they had seen drunk people before and that they would ask if they wanted to know anything. He also decided that he'd tell the truth if they asked. As soon as he decided that, one of them asked if he had gone into the house.

"Yes, I did. I could see him from the door, and he appeared to be talking to himself. When I came in, I could see that he'd been drinking. He said something to me, and, to be honest, I got sick and had to crawl back out. I …" Just before he gave all the details the female officer interrupted him.

"I can certainly understand that," she said softly. "Without going into too much detail, I almost lost my dinner when I went in."

Jonathan decided they had all talked about it enough. Apparently, they had decided the same thing because no one said anything else until the ambulance arrived. After a few minutes inside, the EMTs brought Robert out on a stretcher. One of them came over to talk to the officers. He had a Hispanic accent but Jonathan didn't hear him say his name. The angle of the light from the ambulance cast a shadow on his face so Jonathan couldn't see his face or his nametag.

"He is seriously drunk!" the EMT said. "We are taking him in because he's losing consciousness. He may be in danger of alcohol poisoning. He said something about a girlfriend, we think. He's hard to understand. Is she here?"

"No," Jonathan replied. "He beat her up and she's at my mother's house. I'm honestly not sure how she got there."

"Does she need an ambulance?" the EMT asked.

"I don't know, I left pretty quickly and came here. Mom would call if she needed one, though. They were together when I left." Jonathan became very concerned about Ashleigh and began to feel guilty. He had come here because he wanted to, and not because he thought about her needs. Once again, his anger had taken over and he had made a hasty decision. "I'd like to go and check on them."

"Go ahead," the officers said almost in unison. Then the female officer added, "We will probably need to talk to her since we know this has a domestic violence component."

As soon as the ambulance moved, Jonathan got into his truck and started for his mom's house. While he drove he thought about Ashleigh and his mom. He couldn't remember asking either of them if they were okay or needed anything. He'd gotten angry and left. He thought he should probably apologize when he got back. That shouldn't be long now.

* * *

Waiting for Jonathan made Samantha nervous. She had worried about him from the time he left. She made herself busy working on Ashleigh's injuries and bloody clothes. After a couple of icepacks and some washing, Ashleigh's eye looked worse but she said it felt better. Her nose and lip had stopped bleeding but Samantha could tell they still hurt. In the first hour after Jonathan sped off Samantha had helped her clean up and had offered her some clean clothes. They didn't fit, but she could change back into her own clothes after Samantha washed and dried them. Samantha kept looking out the window and pacing. She just couldn't be still for more than a moment.

"Are you all right?" Ashleigh asked.

"Yes, but I'm very nervous," Samantha replied honestly.

"Me, too," Ashleigh said. "I hope he'll let me come home. He was really mad this time."

"Wait! You mean this has happened before and you are considering going back?" Samantha couldn't believe what she heard.

"Well, yes." Ashleigh's simple response sounded like there could never have been a question. "He loves me and he really needs me, but sometimes I just make mistakes. See, this was really all my fault."

Samantha stared with her mouth and eyes wide open. She waited for Ashleigh to explain the joke, but she never did. Samantha's vision blurred as the tears began to form. *Oh my God,* she thought, *this poor girl thinks all of this is normal.* Then Ashleigh said something that really broke Samantha's heart.

"Besides, where else would I go? Nobody wants someone who messes up as much as I do. Robert says that he wouldn't keep me around if he didn't love me so much. And I know he needs me. He only hits me if I make him mad by doing something stupid." Ashleigh's brokenness became even more evident when she continued, "A girl like me has to take whatever man will have her. What other choices do I have? I guess I'm lucky to have a man."

Absolute shock overwhelmed Samantha. She couldn't talk or even move. Disbelief is too small a word to describe how she felt. Never, in her whole life, could she remember seeing such a damaged person as Ashleigh. She had so much potential and such a great future. No one had more love to give or more compassion to offer in a relationship. She had become almost invisible to the world by hiding in Robert's shadow of abuse. Before that, many of the little girls in the neighborhood had seen her as a role model. When she wasn't looking, they would try to walk like her or talk like her. They got excited when she said hello to them. Samantha had watched them many times.

Samantha stood motionless and silent until she heard footsteps outside her front door. She didn't have time to think or respond before the door opened and Jonathan stepped into the middle of the room.

* * *

Samantha let out a short but loud gasp that made Jonathan and Ashleigh jump. Jonathan turned toward her and could see tears in her eyes as she ran across the room to him. She threw her arms around his neck and hugged him so tightly he thought he'd choke. Then she whispered in his ear so Ashleigh couldn't hear her.

"Please tell me you didn't." Her voice cracked and she had to steady herself. Then, very slowly, she said, "Please tell me you didn't kill him."

"I sure wanted to, but I didn't touch or harm him at all," he whispered back to her.

Samantha screamed, "Oh, I'm so glad!" She began to cry as she held him even tighter. Jonathan had no doubt that the words echoed all the way down to his toes. It would take a few minutes for the ringing in that ear to stop.

Jonathan's attention turned to Ashleigh, who sat motionless on the sofa. She looked like a frightened child who had learned not to speak unless spoken to. In a flash of revelation, Jonathan knew the whole situation. He had seen Robert as a predator and aggressor. Having known Ashleigh almost her whole life, he could see her brokenness. He could clearly see the defeated victim she had become. He knelt down in front of her and put his hand on hers.

"I'm sorry I left so quickly. Are you all right?" he asked as softly as he could.

"Oh, I'll be fine. This kind of stuff heals pretty quickly on me." If he hadn't been able to see her face he might have thought that she had burned her finger on a pot or scraped her knee. When she continued, her words shocked Jonathan as much as they had shocked Samantha. "I just hope he will let me come home again."

Jonathan felt his own heart break as he heard the words. He looked into the eyes of the girl he had grown up with, hoping to reassure her. But, somewhere behind those eyes, that girl had retreated to a deep hiding place within herself. She didn't look back at him. The shallow frame that held his friend looked familiar to him. She still looked like Ashleigh on the outside. But she no longer filled that frame and bubbled out as she had done before. He didn't see the Ashleigh on the inside. Jonathan could see that the damage to her spirit exceeded the damage to her face. Ashleigh couldn't recognize the poison of abuse that kills the person's emotions long before the body dies. Somewhere inside her own body, Jonathan knew Ashleigh had begun to die.

Jonathan decided not to tell her everything that had happened. She seemed to be in a state of shock, so he went into the kitchen to talk to Samantha. She stood at the sink washing dishes.

"Mom, she seems so...so..."

"Damaged? Injured? Distant?" Samantha interrupted and offered her observations. "She is. All of those and more."

"I've heard about abuse like this before, but I've never been so close to it. I've got to do something, but I have no idea what to do!" Jonathan's voice seemed to get higher as he spoke. The frustration and concern turned to tears and filled his eyes. When he blinked so that he could see, a tear ran down each cheek. He put his palms to his chin while wiping his eyes with his fingers. He seemed to growl briefly, and then he asked, "Do you have any ideas?"

Samantha stopped washing the dishes and turned to face him. "We may never understand what's going through her mind. She may not understand what's going on in her own mind right now. It seems obvious to us that she's not seeing things clearly, but, to her, that's all that she can see." Samantha's curiosity wouldn't let her keep talking without asking, "Jonathan, what happened when you went over there tonight?"

Jonathan briefly told her about his thoughts as he drove and the rage that he felt. Then he told her about entering the house and listening to Robert's drunken babble. He decided not to tell her all the details about how he had reacted and what he thought about himself. He'd talk about that later when they could have a longer, more private conversation. Right now, Ashleigh was the main priority.

Samantha listened patiently. She seemed to want to ask or say something twice, but stopped herself. Jonathan finished by telling her about the ambulance and what the EMT said about taking Robert to the hospital. "Do you think we should tell her that he's there?" Jonathan wondered.

"I think so," Samantha answered. "I think she should go to the emergency room herself. Should we report it to the police?"

"In a way, I already did, informally," Jonathan replied. "Somebody really needs to get her away from him or lock him up. Something needs to –"

A gentle but firm knock on the front door interrupted them. When Samantha opened the door, Jonathan saw the same two officers who had talked to him earlier. The female officer spoke first. "Ms. Timms? I'm Officer Tara Miller, and this is my partner Ray Staff. We need to talk to Ashleigh Cole, if she's here, please."

Samantha opened the door and stepped out of the way so they could see Ashleigh. She spoke to them from the sofa where she lay curled up with a blanket. "Hello, again," Ashleigh said. "What is it this time?"

Officer Miller crossed the room and sat on the sofa near Ashleigh. "That's what we need for you to tell us." She smiled as she said it. "It seems like maybe there is something going on that we need to know about. What happened to your eye?"

Ashleigh began to answer with a rambling lie. "I accidently walked into the door at our apartment and hit my eye. You know how sometimes you can be so clumsy. I was just getting back from the grocery store and I had bought some groceries and I guess Robert didn't see me come in and when he turned around he hit me with his elbow some kind of way. It was an accident and really all my fault." She talked so fast that they had a hard time understanding what she said. Officer Miller had heard this kind of story before.

While they were talking Jonathan made eye contact with officer Staff. With only a slight nod, Officer Staff let Jonathan know that he had done the right thing when he let them know what had happened and where they could find Ashleigh.

Officer Miller took out her notepad and began to ask Ashleigh more questions. Samantha and Jonathan stood behind Ashleigh and a few steps away. They could see both officers' faces but they couldn't see Ashleigh's face. She retold her story about the events of the day, but this time she spoke slowly and truthfully. Officer Miller told Ashleigh what they knew about Robert's trip to the hospital. After a few more minutes of questions and answers, and after the officers had written several pages of notes, they closed their notebooks and started for the door.

"Do you have a cell phone, or can you tell us where you will be tomorrow if we have more questions?" they asked Ashleigh.

Samantha and Ashleigh had already talked about this, so Samantha answered. "She lost her cell phone, but you can reach her here. I'll be with her so you can use my cell phone number." She wrote it on small sticky notes and gave one to each of them.

Officer Staff paused on his way out the door and turned toward Ashleigh. "This is not a legal order, but fatherly advice. You need to talk to someone, a counselor or pastor or something." He looked at Jonathan and Samantha, then back at Ashleigh. "Because he's probably going to kill you next time. I have seen this kind of situation before. I know you don't believe it, and you think he's not that way, but at least think about it." He looked straight into Samantha's eyes this time while he continued his plea. "Please, I have worked these cases before."

Samantha nodded and his eyes went back to Ashleigh. She smiled and said, "Okay."

No one said anything until they heard the officers' car start up and leave. The events of the day had left them all exhausted. Ashleigh excused herself and went to the bathroom. Jonathan went to the kitchen to get a glass of water and Samantha followed him. "Do you want to stay here tonight?" she asked in her motherly voice.

Jonathan smiled. "If you need me, I will. If not, I'll go home and clean up. Then I need some sleep. I have to work long hours for the next few days, but I really want to talk to Jimmy. He's helping me so much."

"I can tell. Spend all the time with him that you can. And I always want you to stay here when you want to, but I don't need you to. I will talk with Ashleigh and take her where she needs to go tomorrow. I think she needs some girl time." She hugged him and said, "And I think you might need some Mama time soon!"

"Yeah," he admitted, thinking through the events of the day. "Yeah, I really do." He squeezed her and kissed her on the head. Then he turned toward the front door.

Ashleigh walked back into the living room at almost the same time he did. "It was good to see you again, Jonathan."

"It was good to see you, too. If you need anything, let me know. Good night." He gave her a quick hug and reached for the door. Samantha had turned off the kitchen light and stood by Ashleigh.

Jonathan whispered, the same way he had when he was a small child, "Good night, Mom." Then he stepped out the door.

"Good night," Samantha whispered. Jonathan looked back and saw her smile that special mother-smile that always made him feel loved.

Jonathan sat in his truck and watched the house for a few moments before he left. So much had happened today that he had to think about it for a little while. He saw the lights in the house go off. He turned the key, started the truck, and backed out of the driveway.

Chapter 8

I-beam

Weather changes allowed Jonathan to work long hours for the next week. The extra money helped but left no time for any type of social life. He called and talked to his mother some, but the only time he saw her was when she drove by his worksite and waved. He did get the latest news on the Ashleigh and Robert situation.

He learned that Ashleigh had gotten some medical treatment for pain in her eye. The swelling and the bruises were almost gone now. Her doctor said she expected no long-term damage or scars. He also learned that Ashleigh finally listened to Samantha and went to talk to a counselor. Then, she had enrolled in some recovery-type classes.

Officers Miller and Staff arrested Robert when the hospital released him. The domestic violence charge probably would result in some jail time. Thoughts of Robert seemed to camp out in Jonathan's head. Several times a day he'd replay in his mind the sight, sound, and smell of Robert in the chair. Every time he did, he could see himself in the chair. That made him even more disgusted with his own mistakes and bad choices.

The sound of the backhoe drowned out most of the other sounds. The cab became a meditation chamber where he could focus and reflect on his past and future. For several hours each day, Jonathan thought about his mistakes and their consequences. After a long time of thinking about those mistakes, he came to two conclusions. First, most of his mistakes were not accidents. He had intentionally done those things even though they were wrong. After he reached that conclusion, the second one jumped out at him. He and he alone was responsible for every one of them.

Now, he wanted to be a better person. He'd begin with working on his core values. He and his mom were two deciding factors in every decision he made. He and his mom were his first two core values. He really didn't have any other close family or very close friends. Still, he wanted to base his life on more than just himself and his mother. One day he would have a wife and children. They would certainly be core values to him, but he didn't even have a girlfriend now. His old friend group had also been his party crowd. They were no longer a significant part of his life.

For the next few days Jonathan tried to think less about what he had given up, and more about who he wanted to be. He chuckled to himself as he worked Wednesday morning. After working on the foundation of a house for about two hours, he had a thought. *I'm working on the foundation for a house with this backhoe while I'm on a backhoe working on my own foundation for my integrity. With a backhoe. On a backhoe. That sounds like a children's book.* Without intending to do it, Jonathan began to think about reading to his children. One day, he would sit in his chair with a little boy and a little girl on his lap and read them a book. His little boy and his little girl. His son. His daughter.

He paused for the briefest of moments and smiled. For the first time in days, he had thought about himself sitting in a chair and he didn't have the picture of Robert in his mind. He didn't see himself as drunk and disgusting. He saw himself as a happy father and husband in a comforting home. The chair in his mind no longer smelled of alcohol and sickness. This new chair in his mind smelled of baby lotion and fresh baked bread. The Jonathan he saw in this chair smiled and hugged his children. He had hope and a future. He had something better and more important than just himself.

Suddenly this whole "core values" idea made sense. Not just *I know what you're talking about* sense, but real sense. Life changing sense. He would have (he hoped) children that he could read to and teach and with whom he could play. Although he didn't know who his future wife would be, or even if he would have one yet, he had a special love for her. She'd be the mother of his children. And even if he didn't know for sure if he'd really have children, he already loved them and wanted to spend time teaching them.

For every bit of excitement that he had about teaching his children, he had a distinct feeling of fear to go with it. He wanted to teach them to be good children and grow into good adults, but he wasn't sure he even knew how to do that himself. Could he be good enough to teach them that? A sense of gratitude for what Jimmy was teaching him began to swell up inside him. He became even more resolved to learn all he could. Maybe Jimmy could help him know how to pray and God would help him. He briefly thought about praying right there, but he didn't.

Jonathan didn't grow up in church or in an atmosphere where anyone prayed on a regular basis. *I'm pretty sure,* he thought to himself, *that throwing a prayer at God doesn't mean he's going to throw a blessing to you. There must be something else to it. Otherwise, everyone would be driving a new car.* He made a mental note to ask Jimmy about that next time they were together. He wanted to know if he could make God a core value if he never knew about God before. And could a God he had never really known help him to become a better man?

Chelsea called just as he finished digging the last footer for a new house. "Are you finished with the footers yet?" she asked.

"Just finished about one minute ago. What's up?" He knew Chelsea never called him in the middle of a workday unless she needed to tell him about a change of plans. Uncle Steve gave specific instructions for Chelsea to call only for pure business reasons. The calls had to be as short as possible. Otherwise, Chelsea would talk non-stop and no one could get any work finished.

"Mr. Green said to call you and tell you not to go straight to the next job. You're to refuel the truck and backhoe and take a break. For some reason the work on Baldwin Road can't start until after 2:00 and he will meet you there." She had called Uncle Steve "Mr. Green." Jonathan wondered if she was mad or just trying to be professional. She usually called him Uncle Steve, even though they weren't related.

Jonathan found himself still holding the phone after Chelsea had finished. Had she finally learned how to say what she needed to and hang up? Jonathan wondered if she'd still spend hours on the phone with her friends gossiping about other people. He hoped she had matured through that stage. Maybe she had. At least she had finally learned to give brief messages about work details. He decided to refuel and go to Aunt Jo's for lunch. He had been so busy lately that he had been eating his sandwich lunch while working. He could get excited about a lunch that didn't come out of his little cooler. Eating at Aunt Jo's would be a welcomed break.

Less than two miles away he pulled in to the station where he usually filled up the tractors and the spare tank with diesel fuel. Since he had just filled up yesterday this would be a quick refill stop. He could almost taste Aunt Jo's fried chicken.

While he refueled, he could hear three men talking. They looked like they were doing the same kind of work, because they had the same kind of dirt on their clothes. Jonathan thought they might be concrete workers. They sat on crates near the corner of the building in the shade. One wore a cowboy hat, another a baseball cap. The third had a bandana tied around his head that he pulled off and used to wipe his neck. He nodded a greeting to Jonathan while the other two men talked.

Jonathan couldn't hear everything they said, but the two with their backs to Jonathan seemed to be teasing Bandana Man about church.

"So, what songs did you sing at church Sunday?" Cowboy Hat asked as he laughed and punched Baseball Cap with his elbow.

"I bet your wife made you go again, didn't she?" Baseball Cap said.

Jonathan decided, from what he could hear, that Bandana had attended a church last weekend with his wife and now he appeared to be inviting them to attend as well. One seemed to think attending church showed weakness. The other thought that letting your wife tell you what to do on the weekend showed weakness.

Jonathan overheard Cowboy Hat say, "That church stuff might be all right if you're weak. I don't really need it myself."

"It's not a matter of being weak," Bandana Man responded. Jonathan couldn't hear the rest of what he said.

Then Baseball Cap took his turn to poke fun, "My wife don't tell me what to do with my weekends. I work hard and I make my own decisions."

When Jonathan finished pumping, he had heard just enough of the conversation to be curious. He wondered what the Bandana's response would be. He glanced toward the three and found himself looking into Bandana's eyes. He almost expected the man to be making excuses or to be embarrassed, but the man looked past his two friends and straight at Jonathan. He smiled as if he knew something the other two didn't and nodded slightly at Jonathan.

Jonathan nodded in return and climbed back into his truck. He decided Bandana had gone to church because he wanted to, and not because his wife had made him. Jonathan also got the distinct impression that nothing about the decision had anything to do with weakness.

Driving to Aunt Jo's Diner gave him time to think. He wanted to talk to Jimmy about a few things. He really wanted to get Jimmy's input on the Ashleigh situation. He needed Jimmy to help him sort out his feelings about Robert, too. When he looked at the clock on the dashboard he thought about his last trip to Aunt Jo's with Jimmy. *The timing might be just about right for Jimmy to be there now, if he eats there today,* he thought. *Maybe I'll catch him.*

When Jonathan entered Aunt Jo's he saw Jimmy at the same table where they had eaten before. He faced the door but didn't look up when Jonathan entered. His focus seemed to be on one of the tables to his right. Jonathan looked to his left and located the source of Jimmy's interest. Ashleigh sat with her back to the room talking to Aunt Jo. The noise level in the room drowned out the conversation, and Jonathan could hear nothing they said. Aunt Jo's face showed all the emotions of a mother telling her child she couldn't play in the street. A balance of love and firmness flowed with every word and expression.

Then Jimmy noticed Jonathan and waved. He motioned for Jonathan to join him. Jonathan made his way through the tables and chairs to sit with Jimmy. After they shook hands Jonathan sat down, but neither spoke for a few moments. They both watched Aunt Jo and Ashleigh.

"How long have they been talking?" Jonathan wondered aloud.

"A long time. At least through two waves of the lunch crowd." Jimmy smiled as he answered. "Kayla and Joy have been working double time."

Aunt Jo did more ministry and counseling in her diner than many pastors and counselors do in their offices. The wisdom of age and experience coupled with her compassion made her a wonderful listener. Her advice sounded simple but bore the wisdom of many experiences. Basically, she told everyone the same thing. "Do what you already know you should do." Sometimes she gave the "you're a special person" lecture. Sometimes you could catch a glimpse of her praying with someone.

Jonathan saw Kayla across the room and she smiled at him. She pointed to a plate with chicken and some vegetables and raised her eyebrows as if to ask a question. Jonathan nodded and they both knew he had just placed his order. Less than a minute later, Kayla stood at the table with his food, drink, silverware, and another smile. The plate held three pieces of chicken and vegetables piled high. She had also brought a bowl of potatoes with gravy and a tall glass of iced tea.

"You haven't been in here for a long time, so I figured you'd be really hungry," Kayla said. "Dessert is cherry pie. Wave when you're ready."

Jonathan started to answer but she had already gone to another table. His attention returned to Aunt Jo and Ashleigh. "I wonder what they are talking about so seriously. Does Aunt Jo know about the abuse?"

"She's known about it for a long time." Jimmy's answer had a note of sadness in it. "Ashleigh keeps going back to Robert or waiting for him to come back to her. She won't recognize the special treasure that she is. She's becoming a vocational victim."

Jonathan had never heard that term before so he looked at Jimmy in surprise. A mouthful of chicken kept him from asking what he meant, but Jimmy seemed to sense his confusion and responded.

"That's just my unprofessional name for it." Jimmy explained. "She seems to feel a calling to be the victim. She has chosen the lifestyle of letting herself be abused. Predators like Robert seem to lure victims in and take advantage of them. She stays because she gets attention. The attention is negative, but negative attention is better than no attention, at least in her mind. In a way, they're both trapped. Neither will ever be happy in that situation. Right now, Jo is giving her half of the Respect Talk." He looked across the room at Aunt Jo, and Jonathan thought he saw her wink at him.

Jonathan had swallowed and could ask his question this time. "The Respect Talk? Isn't that what you told me before that we would talk about later?"

"Part of it," Jimmy said. "I'm impressed that you remembered that specifically."

"Man, you just don't know how much I *am* listening. The things we talk about echo around in my head for days after we talk." Jonathan laughed as he finished. "You'd be surprised how many times I hear your voice over the motor on the backhoe."

"I'm glad," Jimmy said with a look of genuine concern in his eyes. "So many people don't want to change at all. I have a strong desire to pour my life into other people, but sometimes they won't accept it. Some want me to pour myself into them, but they seem to have their cups upside down, if you know what I mean."

"I sure do," Jonathan said between bites. "I have been that upside down – or broken – cup most of my life. I'm right side up now, and I'm not leaking that I know of, so pour away."

Jimmy's passion glowed as he began to talk. "You know about building, so you understand the concept of core values and foundations. There are four Cornerstones of Integrity that rest on that foundation." Jimmy stopped when Jonathan held up his index finger as if he wanted to say something. He had to swallow before he could speak.

"I'm sorry to interrupt, but I have a question about the core values thing. I have been thinking about our conversation about God and church. I had decided I really do want to make God one of my core values, but I have no idea how. Then I heard some men talking when I was on my way here this morning and they seemed to think that needing church is a sign of weakness. It was almost like they thought that real men don't need God, or at least, don't need church." Jonathan finished the bowl of potatoes while Jimmy thought for a moment and then answered.

"Did you come to any conclusions about their thoughts?" Jimmy decided to let Jonathan share his thoughts first.

Jonathan stacked his plate and bowl together and cleaned up his eating area. Just as he finished, Kayla returned with his check and refilled his drink. He turned to Jimmy and began to share his thoughts. "I did. I decided to look at the whole picture as if it was a house or building, you know, like the illustrations you've been using."

Jimmy smiled and leaned forward a little in his chair. Jonathan could tell he had Jimmy's total attention. He looked into Jimmy's eyes and continued, "Early last year I helped Uncle Steve do some work on his house. I'm not sure what the source of the problem was, but the floor in his house had begun to sag down. It got really bad in the middle of the house. When I first looked at it, I thought he was going to have to move. The floor dropped some and began to pull away from the walls. In one room, you could slide your cell phone under the wall into the hallway. The floor felt like it bounced in parts of the hallway."

"That sounds like a big enough problem to make you want to move," Jimmy said thoughtfully.

"I think the place where the house was built just settled over time, but I'm not sure. Anyway, the problem was the foundation. It needed strength. To fix it we dug extra footers on each end of the house and ran a big chain under it. Then we attached the chain to this huge I-beam that Uncle Steve had ordered. One of his engineer friends had it designed for him. Then we hooked the tractor to the I-beam on one end and pulled it while we pushed it from the other end with the backhoe. When we got it in place, we jacked it up to the right level and set it in place on the footers. The floor came up to meet the walls and the house was solid. No more bouncy floors!"

Kayla came by the table and picked up the check and the cash Jonathan had laid on it. Jonathan indicated that any change would be her tip. She smiled the Kayla-smile that everyone loved so much and whispered a quick, "Thank you" as she hurried toward the kitchen.

Aunt Jo and Ashleigh still sat and talked at their table. Some of the customers were leaving and others coming in, but more were leaving than entering. The lunch rush seemed to be over. Jonathan glanced at the clock near the counter and noted that he still had time to talk. Jimmy glanced toward Aunt Jo's table again. Jonathan wondered what he was waiting for and Jimmy noticed his puzzled look.

"I'm sorry. Jo wants me to talk to them when they finish, and I am trying to be available. I am listening to you, though." Jimmy explained. Then he asked, "How long did it take to get the I-beam in place? I bet it was heavy!"

"I have no idea how much it weighed," Jonathan answered, "but it took all day to get it in place. I mean a construction crew day, not a banker's day. We started at dawn and I left just before dark."

Jimmy's eyes glanced at Aunt Jo and Ashleigh again. Jonathan wondered how long they'd been there and how much longer they would stay. He found himself relieved that Ashleigh finally seemed to be listening to someone. He couldn't hear anything Aunt Jo said, but Ashleigh seemed to be soaking up every word. Jonathan found comfort in the idea that Jimmy might be talking to Ashleigh.

When Jimmy looked back, Jonathan continued. "When I thought about the I-beam, I remembered thinking that the house looked fine from the outside. When the contractors built the house, the foundation couldn't handle the long-term weight and stresses the house faced. No one knew how weak the house really was until years later when weight and stress made it clear. When I was a little boy, I didn't recognize the need for a God-sized strength. So, I guess you could say that I have concluded that I need an I-beam. Maybe even those guys at the gas station do, but they just don't know it yet."

Jimmy stared into Jonathan's eyes. He didn't say anything and he didn't move. His eyes didn't glance toward Aunt Jo. He just stared at Jonathan. Thinking that he might have been completely wrong, Jonathan became suddenly unsure of himself.

"Maybe. I think. I don't know." Jonathan shrugged his shoulders and became silent.

"Jonathan," Jimmy started slowly, "that is probably the best illustration of the need for God in a person's life I have ever heard. I never heard a better illustration, even in my seminary days."

Jonathan smiled, excited about finally understanding so well. Then, his brow wrinkled and his mouth twisted. His gaze shifted from side to side. He still wanted to know how to "add that I-beam", but found himself totally without words for the question. He inhaled to say something a couple of times and stopped. Finally, he asked the only way he knew how.

"How do I make God a core value?"

Jimmy reminded Jonathan about their conversation about God. "You remember when we talked about this a few days ago?" he asked.

"I remember some of it, but I don't think it all soaked in too well. I do remember something about getting to know God and getting to know new friends being very similar." Jonathan still had the napkin with the CIRCLE-F notes on it, but he couldn't remember much of the God part of that conversation.

While Jonathan thought for a second, Jimmy opened a napkin and started searching his pockets for a pen. Kayla walked quietly by, placed a pad and pen on the table and said in a whisper, "From Ms. Joy." She disappeared before either of them could respond.

Jimmy reached for the small pad of paper and a pen that had appeared on the table and looked toward the checkout register. Joy winked at him, and he nodded. Then, he began to give Jonathan some Bible verses to help him and wrote each one down as he referred to it. "The most important beginning part for you is to know that *you* are already one of *God's* core values. In other words, God loves you. That is John 3:16. And everyone does need help, like you said. That's Romans 3:23. God provided an answer for us before we even recognized we had a problem. That's Romans 5:8. God gives His Spirit to become the I-beam holding our weak floor up. That's Romans 8:26."

Jonathan noticed that he smiled when he referred to the I-beam. He also noticed that Jimmy's attention focused in the direction of Aunt Jo and Ashleigh, who seemed to be finishing their conversation. They had their hands clasped on the table and their eyes closed. Jonathan thought they might be praying.

"I told Jo that I would be available to talk when they finished. I hope you don't think I'm rushing to get away from you," Jimmy said as he finished writing on the notepad. "I don't know whether you have a Bible or if you know what these references are. The Bible is a collection of books. Each book is divided into chapters. The chapters are divided into verses. The first part of the reference, like John, is the book. So John 3:16 means the book of John, the third chapter and the sixteenth verse. The table of contents in the front of the Bible tells you what page the book starts on."

Jonathan saw Aunt Jo motion to Jimmy, who nodded back to her. Jonathan also noticed the clock and realized that he didn't have time to wait, even if Jimmy did. He accepted the note and shook Jimmy's hand.

"I'm sorry to cut us off, Jonathan, but I have to go. Let's get together again soon. If you don't have a Bible, stop by the office and Angie will give you one. I'm proud of you for working so hard on your life changes. Study these and think about how to apply them in your life."

"Thanks, I'll call you tomorrow, and I have to hurry to work, too," Jonathan said. He went toward the restroom as Jimmy headed for Aunt Jo's table. When Jonathan returned to the dining room, he saw Kayla clearing the now-empty table where Aunt Jo and Ashleigh had been sitting.

As Jonathan left the diner, he saw Jimmy and Aunt Jo walking slowly across the parking lot and talking to Ashleigh. He would've liked to speak to her, but he could see that he didn't need to interrupt. He watched them walk and talk for much longer than he had intended. While he walked slowly to his truck, all his thoughts focused on Ashleigh. He hoped she would get the help she needed. He also wondered if she had seen him in the diner.

Chapter 9

Hope for Ashleigh

Ashleigh hadn't seen Jonathan enter or leave the restaurant. In fact, she'd hardly noticed anyone. She'd been at the diner since Samantha brought her to meet Joy just after the breakfast crowd left. She and Samantha had talked to Joy and Aunt Jo at the counter. Kayla took care of the remaining customers, refilling their coffee and removing the dirty dishes. Ashleigh and Samantha gave the updates from the last couple of weeks while Joy and Aunt Jo listened attentively. Finally, Ashleigh said something that really seemed to catch Aunt Jo's attention.

"But, all things considered, my life is pretty good except for this little bump. I'll be home soon and everything will be back to normal," Ashleigh said. Anyone listening could tell that she hoped she could convince herself. They all knew that she didn't ever need to go back to that home situation.

Aunt Jo didn't let Ashleigh's statement go unanswered. "Ashleigh, you don't need to go back to that kind of normal. No one deserves the treatment you've been getting. You deserve so much more."

"Not me," Ashleigh responded in a muted voice. "I don't deserve anything. I'm just an alcoholic: a drug-addicted throw away." She attempted a laugh to make it sound like a joke, but she had finally made the true confession in public. She surprised herself and everyone else. No one expected her to admit her addictions, not even herself.

Samantha and Joy had hoped that Aunt Jo would have an opportunity to talk to Ashleigh privately about her life. They had planned to get her here for that reason. Jimmy had accepted their invitation to meet them here so he might be able to talk to Ashleigh, or get her to talk to Aunt Jo. Not one of them thought Ashleigh would open up and talk, but they were hopeful. Now, she had almost invited Aunt Jo to enter her private world. Aunt Jo cared far too much to let the invitation go unanswered. She could walk right into Ashleigh's world and sit down.

Aunt Jo's mother instinct showed itself when she firmly but lovingly said, "Ashleigh, honey, there are no throw away people in this world and certainly none in my diner. Come over here and sit with me a few minutes." They left the other women at the counter and chose a table by the window. Ashleigh sat down in Aunt Jo's Diner while Aunt Jo sat down in Ashleigh's heart.

As they sat down, Ashleigh explained, "I don't know why I said that. I have never admitted that, even to myself. But I guess it's true."

"No, it's *not* true," Aunt Jo said, her mother-voice still strong. "Now, you may have alcohol and drug addiction problems. I don't know about that. What I do know is that you're *not* a throw away person. No one is. Look around this diner." She motioned to the small groups of customers who had started filling up some of the tables. "Everyone in here has problems and everyone in here has made mistakes. Not a single person in here is perfect: Jimmy in the back, Preacher Self in that corner, me. We've all made mistakes. But none of us are disposable people."

"I sure do feel like one," Ashleigh said bluntly.

"Ashleigh, honey, listen to me," Aunt Jo started. "I know you don't like yourself right now because you've grown comfortable with the idea that you have no value."

"That's why my mother left me," Ashleigh interrupted. "She didn't want me because I was nothing."

"You think that your mother left you because you have no value?" Aunt Jo asked in disbelief. She raised her voice so much that the people at the tables around them got quiet for a few seconds. When they started their private discussions again, she continued. "You're wrong. I knew your mother. The fact that your mother left you has nothing to do with your value. It has to do with her decisions and her integrity, but we can talk about that another time. You have great value and purpose. You think that your addictions to drugs and alcohol take away your value. You're wrong. But the drugs and alcohol will keep you from reaching your full potential."

Ashleigh said nothing but kept looking at a spot on the table in front of her.

"I understand your thinking, though. And I know that you didn't fully hear all that I just said. What registered with you was the two times I said you were wrong, and that made you feel worse. You don't want to admit it, though. You don't want to admit that you can feel. You think that you're worth nothing, so it doesn't matter what people say since you probably deserve it. That's why you let Robert beat you up with his hands and tear you down with his words. You think you deserve it. But it does hurt, and you try to cover the pain with alcohol and drugs. Am I right?" Aunt Jo stopped and waited for Ashleigh to respond.

The wisdom, tenderness and compassion in Aunt Jo's voice seemed to capture all of Ashleigh's attention. Somehow, the words of the older woman seemed to touch her soul. How could someone she'd known for such a short time know so much about her? As Aunt Jo talked, Ashleigh heard the unspoken words of her own broken heart coming from someone else's mouth. She didn't listen; she absorbed. Aunt Jo seemed to understand everything Ashleigh felt, and even some things she didn't know she felt.

"I guess you're right, kind of," Ashleigh answered. Her shoulders stooped a little more and her head bowed closer to the table.

"Well, you do have value, and you don't deserve that treatment. Answer this for me. If you were baking a cake, and I knew you were putting something wrong in the mixture, would you want me to tell you?"

"Yes," Ashleigh answered, and then looked up until her eyes met Aunt Jo's. "But I would want you to tell me what was right, too."

"Exactly!" Aunt Jo said with a smile. "You're putting the wrong ingredients into building Ashleigh, and I want to help you. I want to show you that you have value. I'm not just going to tell you; I'm going to prove it to you. Are you interested?"

Ashleigh sat up straight in her chair. "Sure," she answered. She tilted her head a little to the right and wrinkled her brow. She pressed her lips together and twisted them slightly to the side, which made her nose wiggle a little. When she leaned slightly forward in her chair, Aunt Jo started to explain.

"How much would you say this rock is worth?" Aunt Jo asked as she placed her diamond engagement ring on the table. "Just the rock, not the ring."

Ashleigh knew very little about diamonds. She had pawned a couple but she had never bought one. "I don't know, a few hundred dollars, I guess."

"That's close enough," Aunt Jo said. "How about this one? How much would you pay for this one?" She placed a tiny piece of gravel near the ring on the table. The two stones were almost the same size.

"Honestly, nothing," Ashleigh said. "That's just a rock from the parking lot. Anybody can find all of those they want everywhere."

"What makes the difference between these two stones? Is it just that one is prettier than the other?" Aunt Jo continued her questions.

"Diamonds are harder to find. They're rarer than gravel," Ashleigh answered.

"So, if it's rarer, it has more value?"

"Pretty much," Ashleigh said, her interest growing.

"And what if," Aunt Jo began slowly, "the diamond had a special color and a special cut like no other diamond in the world. What would it be worth?"

"I don't know, but it would be a lot. Probably the most expensive in the world."

Aunt Jo had prepared the next question and began to ask even before Ashleigh finished her answer. "In all the world, in all of the universe, is there another Ashleigh? Is there another you?"

Ashleigh answered with a simple, "No."

"You are absolutely unique. You are the only you. So you have infinite value and infinite worth. There are things that you can do that only you can do. Only you can be you! Don't you see? You are so special!"

Ashleigh's eyes began to fill with tears. She shivered and bowed her head.

"Look at me." Aunt Jo reached over and cupped Ashleigh's chin in her fingertips. "You're too special to let a man, a drink, a powder, or a pill make you treat yourself the way you have been treating yourself and allowing some others to treat you. You think that you're not worthy of anything. You are absolutely worthy. If I decide to throw this diamond ring away, will it still have value?"

"I'll take it," Ashleigh managed to smile. Then she responded, "Yes."

"Then, even if someone like your mother, boyfriend, family or someone else decides to throw you away, you still have value. What if I put chewing gum on this diamond or spit on it? Will it still have value?"

"I guess so," Ashleigh said, "but people might not be able to see it. It could still be cleaned up."

"That is exactly what I was going to say," Aunt Jo agreed. "Even if the value is hidden under addictions or bad habits, you still have value. You and others can more easily see your value, your purpose, and your potential if you clean the junk off the outside. First, you have to realize your own value. Let me teach you a simple sentence that can help you change your view of yourself. Repeat after me and say it with the emphasis that I do."

The sentence that Aunt Jo had made her repeat aloud echoed in her mind. Every different emphasis had its own echo.

I am a person of value and worthy of respect.
***I** am a person of value and worthy of respect.*
*I **am** a person of value and worthy of respect.*
*I am **a person** of value and worthy of respect.*
*I am a person **of value** and worthy of respect.*
*I am a person of value **and worthy** of respect.*
*I am a person of value and worthy **of respect**.*
I am a person of value and worthy of respect.

Although Ashleigh felt strange when she began, she realized that the more she repeated the sentence the stronger she felt. She found herself amazed that the same sentence could be so different with the change in emphasis. She couldn't remember someone actually telling her that she had value. The whole idea seemed strange to her, maybe even too strange. Besides, just because she might think she had value didn't mean she really did. Doubt began to sneak into the back of her mind and the darkness overtook her again.

"I feel better when I say that," she told Aunt Jo, "but just because I say it doesn't make it true."

"That's right," Aunt Jo agreed. "But you aren't saying it to make it true. You're saying it to learn to admit that it's already true. You're a person of infinite value, and you're worthy of respect."

"I appreciate what you're saying, but I know the truth. No one is going to look up to me, especially at this point in my life, no matter how many times I say that."

"The kind of respect you're talking about is what I would call Honor. It's something that you earn. But that's not what I mean. When I say respect, I'm thinking about the definition I learned in class that was taught by a close friend." Aunt Jo looked away briefly, then continued, "Respect is knowing and showing the value of persons and things. That doesn't mean that you expect people to look up to you. It does mean that no one has the right to look down on you! Everyone has value and is worthy of respect."

*　　*　　*

Aunt Jo looked across the room at Jimmy, and winked. He returned her wink. The wink let him know that she would be talking to Ashleigh about respecting herself now. That would be the first part of the Cornerstone of Respect for Persons that he and Jonathan were about to discuss. He turned his attention back to Jonathan and Aunt Jo returned her focus to Ashleigh.

*　　*　　*

Ashleigh confessed, "I don't have a problem admitting that other people have value, but I do have a problem with the idea that *I* have value." She looked at Aunt Jo with pleading eyes and her voice quivered. "What if no one wants the diamond? What if it's only special to one person? Robert is the only one who wants me, and I *need* someone to want me. He's not perfect, but he accepts me. He's willing to put up with me and give me a place to stay. I need him."

"What you need is a new outlook on life. You need to look at yourself from a different perspective. You said Robert 'is willing to put up with me' but you didn't say that he cared about you. I want to hear you say that you have value, and mean it." Aunt Jo gave a hidden nod to Jimmy to indicate that she would soon be ready for him to join them.

"I can try," Ashleigh said as tears slowly began to fill her eyes.

Aunt Jo took Ashleigh's hands in hers and looked in her eyes. "Listen, honey, I care about you, and I'm not just 'putting up' with you. Samantha cares about you and that's why she's letting you stay with her. Many of the people in your life now are really concerned about you. And, on top of all that, God loves you. You asked me, 'What if no one wants the diamond?' You are wanted! God gave Jesus for you, the highest price that has ever been paid for anything. He loves you. I love you. You're definitely worthy of our attention and efforts. I know that it'll be a long process, but will you try to begin to value yourself?"

"I'll try," Ashleigh mumbled. She wanted to value herself and to overcome the challenges in her life. At the same time, she wanted to get high more than she ever had in her life. Only someone who has struggled with chemical addiction can understand the conflict she had in her mind. "But I don't know if I can, and I'm not sure I know how." She expected Aunt Jo to give up on her and to be frustrated. She expected to look at her and see disgust or anger, but that is not what she saw. As she looked into Aunt Jo's eyes she could almost see hope. She started to ask for help, but instead of words only tears and raw emotion flowed out. She cried for a minute while Aunt Jo held her and signaled to Jimmy.

Jonathan and Jimmy rose from the table and started for the door. Jimmy stopped at their table and Jonathan went out toward his truck. Aunt Jo reached out to Jimmy and squeezed his arm. The tears in her eyes and the slight nod told Jimmy all he needed to know about their conversation. Ashleigh stopped crying and wiped her nose and eyes with a tissue.

"Ashleigh, this is Jimmy, he's the friend who taught the class I told you about, and he's a friend of Jonathan. If he can help us find some help for you, are you willing to let him?"

Ashleigh had no words in her response, only a nod and a failed attempt at a smile.

"And I need to ask you," Aunt Jo continued, "if I can tell him all that he needs to know to get you that help. Will that be okay?"

"Yes," Ashleigh consented.

"Jimmy, Ashleigh has been in an abusive relationship for a long time. She has some drug and alcohol addiction problems, and she doesn't think she has any value at all. I think she's almost ready to give up on herself, but *I am not*! Whatever you can do to help us, I'll be grateful for, and so will she." Aunt Jo's compassion saturated her words.

Ashleigh heard something in Aunt Jo's words that she couldn't remember hearing before. She heard compassion, love, and something else. She heard hope and a willingness to share her burden. Many times before people had offered to help, but for the first time she found herself able to hear. The journey to recovery wouldn't be so lonely if someone walked with her. She stood with Aunt Jo and Jimmy and walked through the door and into the parking lot. As she walked, she heard the familiar statement coming from both sides.

"I am a person of value and worthy of respect. Ashleigh is a person of value and worthy of respect. I am…" Aunt Jo and Jimmy continued until Ashleigh began to repeat it with them.

When they neared the picnic area, they stopped. Jimmy faced the two women who stood together, Aunt Jo's arm around Ashleigh's shoulders. He looked into Ashleigh's eyes and spoke gently to her. "Ashleigh, I can help to get you into a rehab center to help you get off the drugs and alcohol. Do you really want to do that? The road will be hard, but we'll walk with you as much as you'll let us. This will mean a life-change, and it'll take a long time. Do you want me to help you get into rehab?"

"I think so, but how soon do I need to let you know?"

"Right now. If you go back to Robert or the alcohol and drugs, you know what'll happen. You'll decide not to get help. Right now, you're in a very tough spot. The drugs you're addicted to are actually abusing you. You're addicted to being abused by the man who's helping you get the drugs. You need freedom from both – the chemicals and the abuser. I know you don't feel strong enough to do this right now, and you probably would love to have a drink and think about it. You don't have to be strong right now. Just admit to yourself that you need help and tell us you want help, and we are here for you. But we will *not* push you. It's your decision."

Ashleigh's eyes filled with tears and her knees shook so much that Aunt Jo had to help her stand. Her voice was strong when she simply said, "Help me."

Jimmy had his phone in his hand before Ashleigh could blink after she asked for help. Starting that day, he arranged for her to get into a detox program at the local hospital and then into a long-term rehabilitation center. She'd need counseling for the abuse and some courses on self-esteem and personal value. The road ahead would be long and hard, but it would definitely be worth the effort. She was worth the effort.

Chapter 10

New Dance Partner

As Jonathan walked toward his truck, he watched Jimmy, Ashleigh and Aunt Jo walk across the parking lot. At almost the same time that Jimmy reached for his phone, Jonathan reached for the door of his truck. Just as he touched the door handle he heard someone call out his name.

"Jonathan, how's it going?" he heard Lexi call out from a few parking spaces away.

He turned his attention to her and smiled. "Great! I'm just working all the time!" he responded.

"I'd like to get together and talk sometime," she stopped before turning between a truck and a minivan to go to her car. She looked quickly at her watch and back to Jonathan. He thought she seemed like she was in a hurry. "But I have to go pay a bill before I head back to work, and I'm running late now."

"I'm almost late for work, too. Again," Jonathan returned. "Want me to text you later?"

"Please do," she answered. "I get off at five today." They waved briefly at one another and Lexi went to her car while Jonathan got into his truck.

Something about Lexi had caught his attention. Her invitation to talk didn't sound like her normal shallow invitation to party or hang out. She sounded like she really wanted to talk. He thought about his old friend group and the times they had spent together. Sometimes he missed them, and the fun. He had come to realize that the fun and the drinking and drugs were not the same. Being with people when you feel a sense of belonging gives you a sense of security.

He had enjoyed the fun and the laughter. He loved the jokes and the interaction. He had almost felt like they were family, but the only common focus was the party life. The group didn't have anything to firmly hold them together other than the shallow fun and the high from the alcohol and drugs. Most families could laugh and enjoy the shallow fun elements while also sharing a heritage from their past or some future goals. That would be a real family, and his heart longed for that.

I must be getting old, Jonathan thought. *I'm starting to think like Uncle Steve.*

As Jonathan began to pull out of the parking lot, he saw Hannah, Samson, Elle, and Sha'qui standing near Omar's car. *Looks like old times,* Jonathan thought to himself. *I wonder where the party will be this weekend.* Sometimes he almost missed his old party lifestyle, but not nearly so much since he had gone to Robert's house. He wondered about his old friends' futures as he looked at each of them. When his eyes fell on Hannah, he immediately thought about how much she reminded him of Ashleigh a couple of years ago.

He wondered how long it would take Hannah to find herself in the same kind of situation as Ashleigh. She had already started down the same road. She had long blonde hair and wore cowboy boots. Everyone knew she thought she was pretty; many would agree with her. Jonathan feared that her focus on external beauty would get her into trouble. She used her looks to get attention, and she used the attention to get drugs or drinks to get high. She liked to party and had chosen the path to self-destruction. Her idea of maturity seemed to revolve around the idea that she had to be different from her parents, whatever the cost. Sometimes she'd choose to do something simply because they would want her to do something else. In many ways, she and Ashleigh were so much alike.

But they were also a lot different. Hannah had family that loved her. Hannah really gave the impression that she loved herself. Ashleigh had neither the love of her family nor love for herself.

Deep down inside, Ashleigh seemed to think she'd never be as good as everyone else. She always seemed to feel like she didn't measure up. Hannah seemed to think she had always been and would always be better than everyone else.

Ashleigh liked to be around people so she'd feel like she was part of a valuable group. Hannah only seemed to like to be part of a group that could give her things. As long as the gifts or compliments came, she could be "happy."

Maybe, Jonathan thought, *Hannah's just selfish enough to never be abused by anyone but herself.*

His thoughts about Ashleigh and Hannah ended when he arrived at Baldwin Road and parked near Uncle Steve's truck. The trailer with his backhoe on it stretched out behind the truck. Jonathan had thought this would be a small job for him, but another truck with a trailer and much bigger backhoe made him rethink. *I wonder who else will be working with us,* he thought as he walked over to Uncle Steve, who stood with three other men. *Whoever it is sure has a nice backhoe.* The shiny green backhoe on the other trailer distracted Jonathan so much he almost stepped on Uncle Steve's foot.

Uncle Steve's "Hey!" brought him back to reality.

"I'm sorry, Uncle Steve," Jonathan started. "I guess I was flirting with the green lady over there."

The small group of men laughed together. Uncle Steve waited to respond until the other men introduced themselves. Jonathan didn't get their last names, but he remembered Joel, Willie, and Bert. Then Uncle Steve completed some of the introductions.

"Jonathan, we'll be doing some work for Bert, here. He needs a retaining wall and you'll dig the footer for that. He also needs a diversion ditch dug at the far end of this lot. We have another job to start the day after tomorrow. Bert wants this all finished before then. Another crew will build the retaining wall. They'll start tomorrow morning. You have to stay ahead of them and you've got to finish by tomorrow evening." Uncle Steve led Jonathan away from the others and began to show him the flags that marked the wall boundaries. Then he gave him the simple, hand-drawn map of the lot and asked if he had any questions.

"Where are those guys working? I'm assuming they'll be helping because there's no way I can finish before tomorrow night. Our backhoe just can't move that much earth in that amount of time. That is, unless you want me to work all night." Jonathan knew the limits of his equipment and how much he could do with the tractor or the backhoe in a given amount of time. He watched the other two men go to their trailer and start working on the trailer hitch on their truck.

"Oh, it *will* be hard, but you have to finish, and they're leaving. They won't be helping you at all." Uncle Steve said bluntly.

Immediately Jonathan's old temper raged inside him. He knew what he could and couldn't do in a day, and what Uncle Steve wanted was impossible. He started to say something but caught himself. Jonathan swallowed hard and tried to swallow the anger and frustration at the same time. If he really wanted to change, he had to be committed to it. Uncle Steve was his uncle and his boss. Jonathan committed himself to respect the authority of Uncle Steve and do his best to complete the job. Then he noticed something he'd missed before.

All the men kept looking at one another and seemed to have some private joke. Jonathan wondered if he had dropped food on his shirt at the diner and quickly checked to see. Nothing there. Was his fly open? Nope, all good there, too. What kept them looking at one another and at him that way? He decided that it had to be something about the job and the fact that they knew Uncle Steve had given him an impossible job. He decided the joke would be on them, because he would finish, even if he had to work all night.

While Uncle Steve, Joel, and Willie were talking and looking at some papers, Jonathan decided to get the backhoe unloaded and start digging. When he reached for the handle to release the tie-downs, Uncle Steve yelled at him. "Boy, what are you doing?"

Jonathan felt his face getting hotter and his hands shook. What had he done to make Uncle Steve act so weird today? He had his back turned to them, so they couldn't see his face. He pounded his fist on the trailer to gather himself before he spun around. He knew they could tell that Uncle Steve was getting to him. For some unknown reason, they all seemed to be against him. Jonathan's whole attitude exploded when Uncle Steve finished his statement.

"You'd better leave these men's backhoe alone. Come over here and unstrap ours. You have a lot of work to do before tomorrow night." All of the men laughed out loud as the reality of the situation began to dawn on Jonathan. Uncle Steve waved some papers at him with one hand and pointed at the green beauty with the other. "We just traded that one in, and you have a new dance partner now." Uncle Steve's round belly shook as he laughed.

If Jonathan had stepped forward, he might have stepped on his bottom jaw. His mouth dropped open and his eyes widened. Uncle Steve would pick on him later and tell him that they thought his mouth opened almost wide enough to park the new backhoe in it. He had never been more surprised. At least, not in a good way. Now Uncle Steve's deadline made sense. And, he wouldn't need the other men's help because the green beauty could handle the extra load. The extra horsepower and the larger bucket meant more work in a shorter period of time.

Uncle Steve walked over to Jonathan. He still wore a smile, but his tone sounded more serious now. Somehow, he also looked older and more tired than usual. "Jonathan, the reason we can afford to make this change is you. You've maintained the old machine and have cared for it like I asked you to. You haven't always made good decisions for yourself, especially when you were off for a few days, but you always took care of my equipment. That kept the trade-in value high, and made the new machine affordable. Jonathan, I'm proud of you, and we can afford to accept some larger jobs now." He handed Jonathan the new key.

"Thank you!" Jonathan replied as he took the key. "I do love my work," Jonathan said with a smile and a sense of pride. "And I'm working on making better decisions for myself." He shook hands with Joel and Willie and thanked them. They all laughed again at Jonathan's surprised response and then they talked for minute. Then Jonathan turned to the new backhoe and offered the key the way one might offer a drink. He bowed slightly and asked, "May I have this dance?" He heard the other men laugh behind him. This time he laughed with them.

When they finished all the unloading and exchanging of equipment and papers, the men said their goodbyes. After Uncle Steve left, Jonathan began working almost immediately. Uncle Steve's words echoed in Jonathan's head all afternoon and evening, "...the reason we can afford to make this change is you...I'm proud of you." The encouragement made Jonathan more determined than ever to change. He thought about all the changes in his life in the last few weeks. He decided that the new equipment would be a symbol of his new life and direction. He'd have to maintain his new lifestyle like Uncle Steve expected him to maintain the backhoe.

As Jonathan worked and the sound of the backhoe drowned out the other noises, he began to think. In some ways he felt somewhat empty and alone. Much of his life as he knew it had changed. His weekend routine, his friend group, and his chemical choices had all changed.

But the changes weren't all negative. He seemed to feel freer than he had ever felt before. He had a life ahead of him that had potential and seemed like an open door. He was already changing, but he had felt the changes in his life speed up when he went to Robert's house and realized that the man in the chair could easily be him in a couple of years. Jonathan almost gagged when he realized again how much he had been working on becoming a Robert.

Jonathan had just finished a short section of the footer and began to move to the next area when he caught movement out of the corner of his eye. He turned and saw Rapunzel standing nearby watching him. At least, the students at college had all called her that. She had sat right in front of him in his English 201 class. It took him a minute to remember her real name. He finally remembered it when he thought about the first time he met her. She had walked up to the table in the cafeteria where he and several of his classmates were eating and introduced herself.

"Hello," she had said in her bubbly manner, "I'm Emilie." Almost without any hesitation, she had continued, "And you should know that I'm a princess." She had taken the chair next to Jonathan and joined them as if she had known them all for years. Within a few minutes, they all felt as if they had been waiting for her all along.

Jonathan and the other students had found themselves drawn in by her attitude and smile. Her long – make that very long – hair and her beaming attitude caught them all off guard. Her blonde hair reached below her beltline and her charm reached into their hearts. Her statement had taken them all by surprise, but her tone hadn't offended anyone. Her attitude seemed to be a "you are all princes and princesses, and since I am too, I can sit here." No one felt belittled by her; they all felt as if she were their hostess and they could continue the dinner party now.

Now this Emilie Rapunzel watched him dig in the dirt. She smiled and waved when he looked her way. Somehow, she immediately put him at ease again, even though he couldn't even hear her. He slowed the motor of the backhoe to quiet the noise, climbed down, and went to speak to her.

"Hey, Rapunzel," he teased as he walked up to her. "What are you doing so far from your castle at this time of evening?" As he said it, he realized the sun had just gone down and people were beginning to turn the lights on in their houses. He hadn't been paying any attention to how long he had worked.

"Hey," Emilie laughed. "That's my castle right over there," she said as she pointed to a nearby house. "I just got home from school and thought I recognized your truck. Then I saw it was you and just thought I would say hello. How have you been?"

"I've been going through a lot of changes, but I'm getting better," Jonathan confessed. "How about you?"

"I'm getting better, too," she smiled. "We sound like Jimmy. He always says he's "getting better." I'll soon be in my last year of college, so I'm pretty excited. Did you finish, or are you still working on your degree? I know you were only going to school part-time the last time we talked."

"I'm taking a short break from school until I decide what I really want to major in. That way, I won't use up all the scholarship and grant money while I'm deciding." Curiosity made him ask, "You know Jimmy?"

"Yes," she smiled and her face seemed to glow. "My Aunt Angie works for him. How do you know him? Have you taken his classes?"

"I guess you could say he's mentoring me, but I haven't officially taken any of the classes. He's really helping me, though. In fact, I had lunch with him today and he wrote some things down for me that I'm going to look up later." He reached in his pocket and pulled out the paper with the references on it. Then, with some embarrassment, he added, "If I can find my Bible."

"Oh, I can fix that for you," Emilie said. "I carry one in my car so I can give it away if someone needs one. If you want it, you can have it."

"I hate to take it since I know I have one somewhere," Jonathan responded.

"Well," Emilie insisted, "you can take this one and give it back when you find yours." She paused for a few seconds, and then said as she walked toward her car, "Or, you can pass it on to someone you know who needs it."

Immediately he saw Ashleigh in his mind. He knew she needed it, but he had no idea whether she'd read it or not. And he had no idea what to suggest that she read. He did know that people like him and Ashleigh didn't read much of the Bible. The book could be so huge and intimidating. He had started at the beginning once, but really didn't see what excited everyone. He didn't see anything life changing in the part that he read, and had no idea how much he'd have to read to find it. He looked at the notes Jimmy had given him. Curiosity made him decide he had worked enough today. He had completed the part Uncle Steve told him to finish before tomorrow, but had kept working because he enjoyed it so much. He turned the backhoe off just as Emilie returned.

"Here you go," Emilie said. "This is my favorite translation and it's pretty good. I hope you like it. I'll be praying that the words come alive for you and that you find what you need when you look up those references."

The honest concern in her voice touched Jonathan. *She really is a princess*, he thought to himself. He started to respond when she added, "I'm sorry, but I have to go in now." She slapped her leg and started walking toward home. "The mosquitoes are coming out and they are eating me alive. I hope you don't think I'm rude, but –"

Jonathan interrupted her, "No, go ahead. I understand. I need to get out of this man's backyard anyway. Thanks for the Bible!" For the first time he noticed the buzzing of the mosquitoes in his ear.

Emilie called back over her shoulder, "I'm glad I had one. See you later." She disappeared behind her car.

Uncle Steve had told Jonathan to leave the backhoe on the jobsite, so he put the key in his pocket and started for his truck. He turned and looked at the backhoe one more time in the fading light. He decided to name her Jade, because of the green color. She had been a good dance partner today, and he'd enjoyed the dance. He realized suddenly that he'd eaten nothing since lunch and that dancing like that makes a man hungry and tired. All of his other thoughts had to get in line behind food and a shower, and he wanted them in that order.

A quick hamburger on the way home took care of the food he needed. He put the Bible on the chair as soon as he walked into his apartment. Then he pulled off his boots, put them in their place by the door, and headed for the shower. A half hour later he had showered, laid out his clothes for tomorrow, made a mental note to wash clothes this weekend, and sat down in his chair with the Bible in his lap ready to read.

He had never seen a Bible with a camouflage cover before. He smiled at the idea of someone like Emilie having one. At least he wouldn't have to try to find one.

He unfolded the paper Jimmy had given him and looked at the notes. He had never used a Bible before and found himself grateful for the instructions Jimmy had given about how to use one.

He paused before he started looking in the Bible or reading the notes and remembered what Jimmy had said. "I don't know whether you have a Bible or if you know what these references are. The Bible is a collection of books. Each book is divided into chapters. The chapters are divided into verses. The first part of the reference, like John, is the book. So John 3:16 means the book of John, the third chapter and the sixteenth verse. The table of contents in the front of the Bible tells you what page the book starts on."

Jonathan looked in the table of contents in the Bible and found the page for the book of John. Then he found the third chapter and the sixteenth verse. Before he read it, he looked at Jimmy's note. *You are one of God's core values. God loves you. John 3:16.* Jonathan's childhood visits to a backyard Bible school hosted by one of the local churches had introduced him to this idea before. The actual words of the section of John 3 that he read carried much deeper meaning than he remembered:

> *16 "For God loved the world in this way: He gave His One and Only Son, so that everyone who believes in Him will not perish but have eternal life. 17 For God did not send His Son into the world that He might condemn the world, but that the world might be saved through Him. 18 Anyone who believes in Him is not condemned, but anyone who does not believe is already condemned, because he has not believed in the name of the One and Only Son of God."*

Jonathan immediately had almost as many questions as he had answers. He remembered some of the story from his childhood exposure in Bible school. God sent His Son, Jesus, to the world to be born in a stable in Bethlehem. Later, Jesus died on a cross for our sins. At least, he seemed to remember it that way. Jonathan began to understand the need for churches and people who could help with these answers. He wondered where Emilie went to church.

Jimmy had the notes written in an outline form. Jonathan concentrated on each part and thought about it before he continued. He decided to match what Jimmy wrote with what the verses said. Jimmy wrote, "You are one of God's core values." The verse said, "God loved the world this way: He gave His One and Only Son."

Jonathan thought about this for a few minutes. *God. THE God. The One who made everything, loves the world. Jimmy said I am one of God's core values. If a core value is something that is as important to me as I am, then God sees me as important to Him as He is. He is willing give Himself as a great sacrifice for me. Jesus died for me.* For a moment, all of Jonathan's thoughts went silent.

Then, Jonathan said aloud to the empty room, "So God loves me so much that He gave a life for me. I should give my life to Him if I want to learn to love Him."

He could almost hear a critical voice in the room say, "Yeah, but you aren't worth having. You've made too many mistakes. God probably doesn't want you."

Jonathan's thoughts immediately jumped to his relationship with Uncle Steve. He had disappointed and hurt Uncle Steve many times in the last years. Now, in the last few weeks, he had grown to love Uncle Steve more than he ever had. He had been living every day trying to pour himself into Uncle Steve's company and to be a part of what Uncle Steve had built. Uncle Steve already loved him and had accepted him, but he'd just begun to understand how to be part of what Uncle Steve offered. Today, Uncle Steve had said the words that still echoed in Jonathan's mind, "I'm proud of you."

Uncle Steve looked beyond all the mistakes and saw the focus and commitment that Jonathan had for him and the company. He thought about the sacrifices that Uncle Steve made over the years to allow Jonathan to keep working with him. Now, he had made a huge investment in the backhoe because he believed in Jonathan. He didn't condemn Jonathan for his past mistakes, but he accepted him for the man he could become. Since he'd decided to change his life and direction, Uncle Steve decided to help him.

He seemed to hear the voice again, saying, "You have made too many mistakes. God will not want you. God is not Uncle Steve."

Jimmy's next note almost seemed to glow on the page. "Everyone needs help, everyone has breaches. Romans 3:23." Jonathan quickly found that verse and read it aloud.

> *23 For all have sinned and fall short of the glory of God. 24 They are justified freely by His grace through the redemption that is in Christ Jesus.*

Jonathan remembered the coffee cups in Jimmy's office. They made the illustration of breaches so clear to him. Now he understood that every person has breaches, but God loves them and has made a way to fix them. "Jesus is the glue that fixes you," he said aloud. Jonathan's excitement pushed him to the next note.

Jimmy had written, "God provided an answer for us before we even recognized we had a problem. That's Romans 5:8." Jonathan turned the page to find that reference.

> *8 But God proves His own love for us in that while we were still sinners, Christ died for us!*

Jonathan smiled. He had drawn the right conclusion. God wants people with breaches, or sins, so He can fix them. He didn't give Jesus because people were good. He gave Jesus Christ to prove that He loved and could fix sinners. Tears began to run down Jonathan's cheeks. A burden that he didn't even know he had seemed to be leaving his heart. As he realized what God had done and continued to do for him, he also began to realize his own value.

Someone infinitely bigger than him loved him. Someone more loving than his mother and more important than anyone he had ever known cared about him. Someone as big as the universe cared about one little breach-filled nobody in a small apartment. God could look past the sin and love the sinner sitting in this chair. Suddenly, more than he had ever wanted anything in his whole life, Jonathan wanted to hear God say what Uncle Steve had said. "Jonathan, I'm proud of you."

The accusing voice still seemed to ring out in the dark corners of the room, "But you don't even know how to pray. You can't get to God. You might as well give up."

Jonathan began to cry. "Oh, God, if you want me, you can have me. You'll have to fix me because I don't know how. I am so sorry for what I have been. I don't even know how to pray, and I don't know how to get to you. God can you help me? What do I do? I feel so weak!"

For the next few minutes, Jonathan cried like he hadn't cried in years. He buried his face in the pillow from the sofa and let all of his emotions flow freely. When he recovered, he looked at the note from Jimmy again. "God gives His Spirit to become the I-beam holding our weak floor up. That's Romans 8:26." He quickly turned the page to the next set of verses.

> *26 In the same way the Spirit also joins to help in our weakness, because we do not know what to pray for as we should, but the Spirit Himself intercedes for us with unspoken groanings.*

Jonathan sensed something new inside. He realized he had prayed, even though he didn't think he knew how. When he released himself to God, somehow God's Spirit had joined him, had come inside him, and prayed when he didn't know how.

Jonathan had a picture in his mind of the security camera at one of the job sites. When Jonathan tried to call the property owner on his cell phone to explain a question, the man had stopped him.

"I can see it all on the security camera, and I hear you on the security monitor," the man had said. Then the man told Jonathan what to do. The owner could almost be in two places at one time, in the office and on the job site. Jonathan sensed something like that had happened tonight. God really could be everywhere, in heaven and in Jonathan. So God knew what Jonathan needed even better than he did.

Jonathan closed his eyes. He belonged to God now. Someone bigger than Jonathan would give him purpose and value. His change was no longer so much about his behavior. Now everything would be about his new identity. Finally, he began to understand the concept of personal integrity on the deepest level. The absolute core of Jonathan changed. He knew, but couldn't explain, that he had become new. The old Jonathan had gone, and a new Jonathan replaced him. He sensed a peace and a love for this God he had never thought much about before. He thought about calling Jimmy, but decided to wait a little while.

A new Jonathan slept in the chair all night with the Bible in his lap.

Chapter 11

New Life Plans

When Jonathan woke up the next morning, he found that his new spiritual life didn't mean the absence of pain or challenge. Emotionally he felt great, but it took almost an hour in the shower to get the tightness out of his neck from sleeping in the chair. Dense fog slowed his trip to the worksite. When he rode past Emilie's house and turned in at his worksite, he noticed that Emilie had already gone back to school. He had hoped to arrive before she left. He felt a little disappointed.

Then he found bird droppings on the seat of his new backhoe. He felt a disgusting disappointment this time. He cleaned off the seat and did all of his routine maintenance checks. Turning the key brought Jade to life. A puff of black diesel smoke drifted off in the wind. He smiled. He and Jade both had new lives and new directions. When he finally started working, he felt like a new man with a new life in every area.

The retaining wall crew arrived just as he finished the last part of the foundation. He waved and moved Jade to begin the diversion ditch. The simple purpose of a diversion ditch is to give water an easy way to get to where you want it to go. Since Jonathan knew where he wanted the water to go, the process didn't take long. In just a couple of hours, he had finished and began to load Jade on the trailer.

Jonathan had just finished securing Jade to the trailer when he got a text from his mom. Samantha didn't call or text him often, and almost never during a workday. When she did, she'd usually text him and ask him to call her later. He couldn't hear his phone or feel it vibrating while working on the large equipment anyway. The text said, *"Call when you can, I have news on Ashleigh."*

News on Ashleigh? What happened? Is she okay? Jonathan felt his heart race and noticed his hands shaking. He decided to call while he took a lunch break between jobs.

"Hey, Mom. What's up?"

"I know you're at work, so I'll be quick," she said. She sounded relieved, even a little excited. "Ashleigh wanted me to let you know that she recognized her addiction problems and has gone into rehab. She will be detoxing for a few days, and then she'll move to the treatment center. She won't be able to call out or receive calls until a month or so after she gets to the center. She can write and get letters, but no texts or email and no phone calls. I have the address if you want it."

"Wow! Yes, I do want it," Jonathan replied. "What made her decide that?"

"I took her to see Joy yesterday morning. Joy and I had talked about Ashleigh's situation a few days ago. Joy told me that we should get Ashleigh to talk to Aunt Jo. I told Ashleigh that I wanted her to meet my friend Joy, who was Aunt Jo's daughter from the diner. She seemed interested, so we went about 10:30. They had called Jimmy because of the contacts he has. They made sure Preacher Self was there too, in case they needed him."

"I saw her there," Jonathan interrupted. "I went to eat and sat with Jimmy. I saw them at one of the tables talking, but I didn't see you there."

"When Aunt Jo invited Ashleigh to sit down, we went into the kitchen," she explained. "We didn't want to be a distraction. Joy is a good person to talk to, and I needed a shoulder to cry on." Her voice cracked and Jonathan thought he heard her sniff a couple of times.

"Are you okay?" he asked. "I can come see you if you want."

"I always like to see you. You know that, but I'm fine. It has been very stressful having Ashleigh here and not knowing what Robert is going to do." Her voice trailed off to a whisper.

Jonathan could hear the exhaustion in her voice. He hoped that she hadn't started drinking again. She had been sober now for a little over two years. He decided to ask. "Mom, you haven't been –?"

"I have not been drinking," she interrupted. "But thank you for caring enough to ask. I have been tempted. I'm going to the Celebrate Recovery support group at Northside Church tonight."

While they talked, Jonathan's phone beeped, letting him know he had another call. "Mom, I have another call, and it may be Uncle Steve or Chelsea. I will call you right back."

"No need to. That was all I wanted. I'll talk to you later. Love you!" she said quickly and the call ended.

Jonathan answered the other call and found Chelsea on the line.

"I didn't expect you to answer," Chelsea said. "I figured you'd be working and wouldn't be able to hear the phone."

"I just finished here and loaded up. What's up?" Jonathan asked as he got into his truck.

"Uncle Steve said to tell you that he knows about Ashleigh and to tell you that Jimmy wants to talk to you. He also said that the weather forecast says rain is coming later today, so you can put the new backhoe in the shop if you want."

"Okay, thanks. What's he doing today?"

"He's sick. He didn't come to the office. He sounded awful on the phone. My other line is ringing. I gotta go."

"Okay, thanks," Jonathan replied. He worried about Uncle Steve sometimes. He seemed to have much less energy than he did last year about this time. He seemed to be staying home more, too.

Jonathan waved good-bye to the other work crew as he pulled onto Baldwin Street and headed for the shop. He decided to drop the trailer off and get some lunch. He had left some chili in the refrigerator at the shop. He'd wait to call Jimmy until after he got there. The first time he hauled new equipment he really liked to drive without distractions. He went over the railroad tracks a little faster than he should have and the trailer movement made him glad he didn't have his phone in his hand. This backhoe and trailer combo affected the truck much more than the other one.

It only took a few minutes to back the trailer into the shop and unhook it from the truck. Then he heated his chili and ate a quick lunch. The quiet shop smelled like dirt, grease, diesel fuel, and chili. "What a mix," Jonathan said aloud as he reached for his phone. He noticed a text he hadn't seen before. It was from Jimmy.

"I'll be at the office this afternoon, and I'd like to talk to you if you can come by," it said. Five minutes and three texts later, they had confirmed a coffee visit for 3:00. Jonathan wondered if Jimmy wanted to talk to him about Ashleigh. He didn't know if he could, because of the private nature of everything. He wanted to talk to Jimmy about his prayer last night and his new commitment to God, too.

"I have a lot to learn," he said aloud. Then he chuckled to himself, "I hope Jimmy's a good and patient teacher."

As he looked around the shop, he began to notice small things that needed cleaning or replacing. Without thinking about it, he began to straighten and organize. Uncle Steve usually reminded him about it before things got as messy as they were now. He wiped the grease from some tools and replaced them in the toolbox. Then he hung the shovel on its peg in the corner, and began to think about Uncle Steve. His little desk in the corner had a cup of coffee on it that had been there for days. Jonathan thought back over the last few weeks to try to remember the last time he had seen Uncle Steve in here.

He decided to call to check on him. Chelsea had been calling Jonathan with his job assignments lately, and he rarely received calls from Uncle Steve. He'd thought Uncle Steve had decided to give her more responsibilities to help her grow. Maybe the company really had grown that much. When he thought about it now, Uncle Steve seemed to be slowing down. When they talked at the jobsite yesterday when they got the new backhoe, Uncle Steve had looked a little more tired than Jonathan expected. While he thought, his fingers dialed Uncle Steve's number.

"Hey, Boy," Uncle Steve picked up on the first ring. He'd seen Jonathan's name on his caller ID, and he always answered Jonathan's calls that way. "What's up? How are you liking the new backhoe?"

"Oh, I love her! She's a great dance partner, and I named her Jade," Jonathan joked. Then he lowered his voice and sounded calm but serious. "Nothing else is really up, I guess. I was just calling to check on you. Are you okay?"

"I'm just really tired, and need some time off. Since you and the other crews had all of the pressing work covered, I decided to take the rest of the day off. Have you finished for the day?"

"Yes, Sir," Jonathan replied. "I'm at the shop and just ate lunch. I'm going to see Jimmy at 3:00, unless you need me for something else."

"No, that's fine. I talked to Jimmy earlier and I know what's going on there. Anyway, you don't have time to start the next project before the rain sets in, so I guess you'll have a little time off."

"Would it be okay," Jonathan almost interrupted, "if I come in tomorrow while it's raining and do some cleaning and sorting in the shop? I noticed a couple of things here that I'd be glad to do tomorrow, if you want."

Uncle Steve made no sound at all for a few seconds. Then, with surprise evident in his voice, he said, "Sure, the shop can use all the cleaning we can give it." This was the first time that Jonathan had volunteered to come in and clean.

"I'll start in the morning, then. Thanks, and get yourself some rest." Jonathan hoped Uncle Steve really would rest and recover. He decided to clean for another hour, then wash up and go meet with Jimmy.

When Steve hung up his phone, he wondered about their conversation. Jonathan had never volunteered to work in the shop before. His tone, and the way he truly seemed to be concerned, impressed Steve. Something really had changed Jonathan in the last few days. He seemed much more considerate and mature than usual. The call from Jonathan relieved some of the stress Steve had been feeling. In fact, it relieved so much stress that he soon fell asleep in his recliner.

While Steve slept and snored at home, Jonathan swept and sneezed at the shop. He even began to sing to himself a little between sneezes. He no longer felt the stiffness in his neck and shoulder from sleeping in the chair. Without thinking about it, Jonathan began to talk aloud to God about Ashleigh and about Uncle Steve. He shared his concerns about each of them. When his phone chimed to remind him of his appointment, he almost felt like it interrupted his conversation.

Washing his hands and closing the shop only took a few minutes. The drive to Jimmy's office took a little longer, but he easily found a parking spot. His excitement grew as he got closer to Jimmy's door. The coffee seemed to smell fresher today for some reason. Angie and Jimmy greeted him as soon as he entered the office. Angie already had a cup of coffee ready for him. He smiled and shook hands with each of them. Then they went into the classroom to sit and talk.

"Jonathan, I talked with Ashleigh yesterday," Jimmy began. "I wanted to talk to you in person because I want you to know what I know so we can talk openly together."

"Mom told me you had talked to Ashleigh," Jonathan replied. "I was hoping I would get to talk to you about her and some other things soon."

"I want you to read this before we start talking," Jimmy said as he handed Jonathan a small piece of paper. It had a note on it in Ashleigh's handwriting.

Jonathan,

> *I wanted to talk to you before I left but I didn't get a chance. Thank you for caring about me and helping me. I told Jimmy he could talk to you about me, and I want you to talk to him. I know confudentialaty is important, so I wanted you to know he had my permision to talk. I will write you when I can.*

Ashleigh

Jonathan smiled. "She never could spell very well." He handed the note back to Jimmy. "I wondered if we would be able to talk. Mom called me and told me that you had talked to Ash and that she was going into rehab. I wanted to talk to you and check on her, but didn't know if you would."

"I wouldn't talk to you in any detail unless I had her permission." Jimmy said. "I wanted her to write you a note so you would know that I had not broken confidentiality."

"I can fully understand. I really appreciate that. It helps me feel better about talking to you about *my* stuff."

Jimmy spoke clearly and slowly. "Ashleigh is going to need a whole lot of support."

"And a lot of prayer," Jonathan added. "I prayed for her earlier. Well, I think that's what you would call it."

"I don't get it," Jimmy's voice showed his confusion. "You think you prayed, but you aren't sure?"

"Yeah. I just kind of talked to God like He was standing there next to me. Did I do it wrong?"

Jimmy laughed. "No, I pray like that quite often. Sometimes I close my eyes and concentrate. Sometimes I keep my eyes open and talk out loud, like when I'm driving. It all depends on where I am and how I feel."

Angie walked through on her way to the coffee pot. She smiled and nodded as he talked, and she whispered, "Me, too!"

Jonathan decided to share about his prayer time last night. "Yesterday after I left you, I saw a girl I knew from one of my college classes. She gave me a Bible. When I got home last night, I read the notes you gave me and looked up the Bible verses. When I started reading, I felt so guilty and worthless. I felt so hopeless. I knew I needed God, but I didn't even know how to pray and didn't know how to get to Him. I kept hearing a voice telling me that I might as well give up." Jonathan wiped a tear that had started running down his left cheek. He sniffed and continued. "I'm sorry, but it's still really fresh in my mind."

"No need to apologize. It sounds like you had a good little study time," Jimmy said as he put his hand on Jonathan's shoulder.

Jonathan smiled. "I wouldn't call it a study. It was more like an invisible adventure. If you had been watching me, you'd say that I never got out of my chair. But, I felt like I wrestled with myself – and with my past. I know you're going to think I'm going crazy, but I could almost feel myself fighting something. It was almost like I could hear a voice telling me that God didn't want me and that I wasn't good enough."

"I don't think you're crazy. It's a common battle that most people fight when they're surrendering to God. I'm not trying to sound overly spiritual, but did you know that the name *Satan* actually means 'accuser' or 'adversary'?"

"So, the devil was trying to get me?" Jonathan half smiled as he looked at Angie.

"No," Jimmy said with a look and tone of total seriousness, "he was trying to *keep* you."

A chill ran over Jonathan's body and it seemed that every hair on his body stood straight up. He shivered as the vivid memory of the night before replayed in his mind. He knew he had somehow been changed by his encounter with God. Now he began to understand just how much he had changed. He had moved from belonging to Satan to belonging to God in the length of time it took to voice one prayer. For a moment he remained completely silent. Angie slipped away and got more coffee for them all. Jimmy patiently and silently waited.

"So, when I told God He could have me but He'd have to fix me, He took it seriously? What it felt like was happening really is what happened?" Jimmy nodded as Jonathan took a few seconds to compose himself. Then he recovered and asked, "What do I do next? Read the Bible?"

"You can *start* reading the Bible," Jimmy said with a slight smile. "And you can *continue* reading the Bible. If you just say 'read the Bible' then it sounds like you read through one time and you have it. One problem with that thought is that the Bible is too big to just quickly read through. Most people get overwhelmed and quit. Another problem is that it doesn't have a simple list of do's and don't's. But I can help you with that."

"I was sure hoping you could," Jonathan said as he looked into Jimmy's eyes. He reached for his fresh cup of coffee and noticed that Angie still sat at the table with them. For the first time she gave her input.

"We all struggle with knowing what to do when we're new Christians. Jimmy's a good teacher, and we'll be here to encourage you. This is not something you have to do all alone. Father tells us that we should not forget to gather with other Christians to get encouragement and accountability."

"That's right," Jimmy added. "The verse she's referring to is Hebrews 10:25. We all need encouragement and we need others to help us know what to do. That's called accountability, and we all need it."

"Man, I sure do," Jonathan interrupted. "One thing I wanted to talk to you about today was how to change. I didn't grow up in church, so I don't know what to do. I need to learn, and I want to learn, but I need help!"

"We all need help," Jimmy replied. "The best starting point for you is to realize that God has changed your *Who*. He's changed your spirit and made you a new person. If you've ever heard someone talk about being 'born again' that's what they were talking about. Now you have to change your behavior. The Mighty King has adopted you, and now you have to learn to live like a prince."

"That goes back to the castle of character thing you were talking about earlier, right?" Jonathan asked. "Where do I start?"

"You're already off to a good start. And we can use the word picture of a castle for our outline. You've started building your castle by setting a good foundation. Your foundation is your core values. Then, we started talking about the cornerstones. We had started talking about the Cornerstone of Respect in here one day. I think it was just before I heard about Ashleigh."

"I remember it was the exact day I heard about Ashleigh," Jonathan agreed. "One of the last things you said that day was that I need to respect myself and treat myself like I have value."

"You have a good memory," Jimmy said. "For personal integrity, Respect can be defined like this: Respect is knowing and showing the value of persons and things. This is different from the idea of honor, like a private respecting a sergeant in the army. What I'm talking about is to show that the person or thing has value. You start understanding this by saying to yourself, 'I am a person of value and worthy of respect'."

"That sounds so simple that you'd think everyone knows it. I would've told you everyone did until I talked to Ash some. I couldn't believe it, but she told me she didn't have any value, that she was worthless. Did she talk to you about that?"

"A little. She and Aunt Jo talked about it for a long time. That's one of the things that helped her decide to go into rehab. She finally started to want to have value. I don't know if she really believes it yet, but at least she wants to." Jimmy looked from Jonathan to Angie.

Angie responded, "We have a lot of students here who don't think they have value. One student who was nearly 60 told us that no one had ever told her she had value until she came here. It's sad, but true. The starting point really is to understand your own value, then to begin to value others. We even had one student who wrote us that she was suicidal when she came, but changed her mind when she realized she had value and hope."

Jonathan spoke next. "So what can I do for Ashleigh, and what is my own personal next step?"

"Until she gets to the place in her treatment where she can get mail, there's nothing you can do directly for her," Jimmy replied. "You can pray for her and for the wisdom to know what to write when she can receive letters."

"I can do that," Jonathan nodded.

"For yourself, begin to intentionally show self-respect. Look in the mirror in the morning and say to yourself, 'I am a person of value, and worthy of respect.' Then say it again and emphasize different parts of the sentence. 'I am a person of VALUE, and worthy of respect.' Jo and I encouraged Ashleigh to do the same thing. This is something I teach in my classes. As you go through the day, think that same way about other people." He turned and faced Angie. "Look at the people you come in contact with and think, 'She is a person of value and worthy of respect.' Then, show that the person has value to you; show the respect you would want for yourself."

"Like not letting the door close in someone's face?" Jonathan asked.

"Exactly. Or holding the door for someone to go first. Cover your mouth and nose when you cough or sneeze. Keep the equipment that you work with clean so it'll last."

Jonathan replied, "It's really neat that you would say that. Uncle Steve just bought a new backhoe for me to use. He said he did it because I took care of the equipment he assigned to me."

"See," Angie said, "you're already working on your personal integrity. You demonstrated respect for the resources he entrusted you with. Respect got you a new ride! You even got ahead of Jimmy! Good job, Buddy!" She offered her hand for a high-five.

Jonathan met Angie's high-five and chuckled. "I even named her Jade, because she's green. I call her my dance partner." They all laughed.

Before they got totally distracted, Jimmy decided to finish the thought about respect.

"The Cornerstone of Respect includes respect for persons and respect for resources. We have touched on each of those a little. The final part to think about is respect for authority." Jimmy and Angie looked at one another briefly before he continued. "Simply put, remember these two things. Submitting to authority does not mean that you have less value. And being in an authority position doesn't mean you're more valuable than someone else. You may have more value to the company or more experience, but every person has value. All persons have equal value, but different functions or roles."

"I get it," Jonathan said. "If I value you as a person, I'll respect the authority you have over me. I won't make it hard for you to supervise me. And if I respect you as a person, I won't use my authority over you as a power play."

"That pretty much sums it up!" Jimmy said as Angie nodded in agreement.

"Speaking of authority," Angie winked at Jimmy and joked, "here comes Ruby."

Chapter 12

What Next?

Jimmy excused himself and went outside to bring in Ruby's laptop and book bag. Even after 30 years of marriage, he still liked to carry her books. Ruby had a master's degree in education but she didn't teach in the school system. Instead, she chose to teach a small, select group of at-risk girls in Jimmy's classroom. Four days a week, she taught four girls. Sometimes she'd stay up until one o'clock in the morning working on lesson plans for the girls. She poured her life into giving them a chance to learn. No one knew yet whether they appreciated it.

"They'll start back to school tomorrow," Angie said. "I think they're going on a field trip tomorrow, but after that they'll be here most days. You can still come by; we'll still be here." She had answered his question before he asked it.

"Good. I wondered if I'd need to limit my visits," Jonathan replied.

When Ruby came in, Angie introduced her to Jonathan. "Ruby Betts, this is Jonathan Timms, Jonathan, this is Ruby."

"Hello, Ruby," Jonathan said with a smile as he shook her hand. "Jimmy has told me a lot about you."

"He has told me a lot about you, too," Ruby responded. "It's good to finally meet you. I understand you're making some huge life changes."

"I am!" Jonathan responded. "But I'm not sure that 'huge' is a big enough word."

As Jimmy came in with Ruby's bags, rain began to fall. In just a few seconds, they were all watching a downpour.

"Well, that came on quickly," Ruby said. "I'm glad I came on in!"

"And I'm glad I'm not working this afternoon," Jonathan replied. "Uncle Steve said the rain would start today and continue for a few days. I love working outdoors, but today's a good day to be inside."

Lightning flashed and thunder boomed. Jonathan thought about the diversion ditch he had finished that morning. Without the new backhoe, he'd still be working on it. He shared his observation with the others as they watched a new river flow through the parking lot.

"We just got a new backhoe. I would've still been working on the job from this morning with the old one. I'm really thankful for the larger equipment. I would've been soaked."

As soon as Jonathan said "soaked" lightning flashed again, the thunder clapped, and the electricity went off. They all jumped and one of the women squealed "OH!" They were all so surprised that not even the squealer seemed to know who made the noise.

"Yep," Jonathan continued after a second, "real thankful."

"Well," Angie offered, "we can't do much else. Who wants to help me drink the rest of this coffee?"

She had already started for the coffee pot before anyone could answer. Ruby, Jimmy, and Jonathan sat down in the waiting area. In just a few minutes, Angie came in with coffee for everyone. Then she sat with them and they talked about the rain and the weather for a while. When the rain slacked off and the sky became a little brighter, Angie began to collect their empty coffee cups.

"I hate to leave good company, but I'm going to head out while it's not flooding," she said with a smile.

"I need to go, too," Jonathan added. "There's probably more of that coming."

"Jimmy," Angie called from her office. "Do you want me to get one of the DVDs for Jonathan to look at?"

"Yes," Jimmy turned to face Jonathan, "if he wants one?" Jimmy answered Angie and asked Jonathan at the same time.

"Sure, I guess so," Jonathan immediately replied. He had no idea what kind of DVD they were talking about, but they both seemed to be excited. He continued, almost trying to convince himself, "It looks like I'll have time. What kind of DVD is it?"

Jimmy answered as Angie brought the DVD and a workbook and handed them to Jonathan. "It's called 'Core Elements', and it's the basic information for all of the personal integrity courses we offer here. We may have talked about it before. It's the one that you can order from our website. The DVD and the *Castles of Character* student workbook are both there."

Jonathan felt excited and reached for his wallet. "How much is it?" he asked.

"You don't have to pay for it," Angie said. "I didn't mean that. This is a gift."

"Yes, I do," Jonathan responded with a smile. "I appreciate the offer, but I'll be more likely to write in the workbook if I don't feel like you loaned it to me. Besides, I know this is how you make your living."

Angie inhaled to give an argument, but Jimmy stopped her by saying, "Jonathan, are you telling Angie that you need to pay for it in order to have ownership in what you're doing?"

"In a way, I guess that is what I'm saying," Jonathan said. "I want to know that I paid for it so that it'll be on the back of my mind that I bought it and need to use it. I guess it's part of my self-discipline. Or lack of self-discipline. I'm not sure which."

Jimmy smiled. "If what you're saying is that you need to pay for it to get the most value from it, I would say that shows integrity. We normally charge thirty-five dollars, but you pay whatever you feel comfortable with. We did intend for it to be a gift." He turned and nodded slightly at Angie and said, "Angie, take the man's money."

Just as Jonathan handed the money to Angie, the lights came back on and the copy machine noisily reset. The refrigerator in the conference room began to hum and the emergency lights turned off. Angie started to laugh.

"It always seems brighter when I'm getting money instead of spending it," she joked. Then she looked at Jonathan. "Jonathan, I wasn't trying to sell you something when I offered you the DVD. I do understand, though. You're certainly a remarkable young man."

The rain began to increase again, so Angie and Jonathan both quickly headed for the door. After waving goodbye, they both drove away. Ruby and Jimmy sat down in the waiting area to watch the rain in silence. None of them saw the black car in the parking lot. A red haired man in the driver's seat watched them as he wrote in his small notebook. When the rain began to pour again, he drove away, completely unnoticed.

Just before Jonathan pulled out of the parking lot onto the road, his phone buzzed to let him know he had a text message. He glanced briefly at the screen and saw that the text came from Lexi. He decided he'd read it when he stopped for a hamburger in just a few minutes. Because of the heavy rain, he went through the drive-thru so he didn't have to get wet. Then, he parked and ate while he read the text.

"Hey! I haven't heard from you since I saw you at Aunt Jo's. Can we talk sometime?"

Jonathan felt a twinge of guilt. He had told her he'd text her later, then he got the new backhoe and totally forgot. "Breach!" he confessed aloud. The loud rain on the truck roof would make a phone call almost impossible, so he decided to text her back. Lexi almost never sent him texts and never called, so he knew she must really want to talk. Since he wanted to make up for not texting her, he decided to offer to buy her dinner the next day.

"Hey! I'm sorry I didn't text you when I said I would. Can I make it up to you by buying you dinner? Maybe tomorrow night?"

Her reply came almost immediately, *"It's a date!"*

A date? That wasn't exactly what he had in mind. He had never thought about asking her out on a date, but he decided it could be fun. Well, it would depend on what she meant when she said that she wanted to talk. He wondered if she might be in some kind of trouble. A bright lightning flash and loud thunderclap interrupted his thoughts. He decided to go home, but to drive slowly. This storm made him want to go home, put on some comfortable clothes, sit on the sofa and watch something on television. He hoped the power would stay on long enough. The sound of sirens in the distance reminded him to drive slowly and carefully.

The rain had slowed by the time he got home. He grabbed his hamburger wrapper and empty cup from his truck and got his phone. Then he ran to his front door. Before he could put the key in the door, he heard someone call him.

"Jonathan! What's up, man?" The voice belonged to Omar. He sat in his car with Edgar and Samson. He had parked just a few feet from

Jonathan's front porch, but on the opposite end from Jonathan's truck, and in the neighbor's parking spot.

It appeared they'd been waiting for Jonathan to get home. He didn't know how to respond for a few seconds because he hadn't expected to see them.

"Hello!" he replied. "I'm just getting home and trying to get in out of the rain. Come on in. What are you guys up to?" He paused. "And what did you do with Pete?"

The rain had almost stopped now, but Jonathan stayed under the cover of the porch while he talked. His three friends got out of the car and came to him.

"Oh, Pete's got a woman on his mind. We were waiting for you. We got an opportunity we want to let you in on," Omar said excitedly.

"We came to bring the lost sheep home," Edgar said as he laughed and slapped Jonathan on the back.

"Yeah, you won't believe this. It's gonna change your life!" Samson said. He carried a case of beer, and Edgar followed him with a small bag.

As Jonathan opened the door and entered, he slid off his boots and encouraged his friends to do the same. They'd been here before, so they knew the drill. Jonathan really tried to keep the carpets clean so he wouldn't have to lose his security deposit when he moved. They had always told him he went too far and often teased him about it. On several occasions, they asked him if he "needed the money that bad." They seemed excited as they began to open the beer and the small bag. Jonathan's eyes widened when he realized the bag held drugs.

"Welcome to the buffet," Samson said as he opened the bag. He waited for Jonathan to move his Bible and papers. Then, he poured the contents of the small bag on the coffee table in the middle of the room: marijuana, a small bag of cocaine, and several kinds of pills. He'd brought enough for everyone. "Already paid for and ready for your pleasure."

"We decided to let bygones be bygones. We've come to help you," Omar began. "We figured that you must have pulled back from us because money was a little tight. We've all been there, so we brought some beer and a few other pick-me-ups to share."

Omar looked to where Jonathan had laid the Bible. Then, he continued, "I saw your Bible on the table there. We brought you some real help, not that fake stuff. You know God don't want people like us. People like you and me could never live up to that church life anyway. And, don't let pride stop you. We know you like to pay your own way, so," he paused as he looked at the other two, nodded and smiled, "we have an opportunity we're going to cut you in on."

Jonathan had never understood the phrase "internal conflict" more than right now. Part of him longed to grab a beer. He wanted to dive into the drugs in the bag and get high with his friends. The fact that he didn't exactly *have* to work tomorrow made the temptation even stronger. Another part of him wanted to scream "what are you thinking?" and throw them all out of the house with the drugs and beer. How could he so intensely want a beer and want to throw it out the door at the same time? How could he want to get high on drugs so much when he had been so high on God just last night? How could he want to be with his friends and want them to leave so badly? The conflicting emotions kept him silent long enough for Omar to begin to lay out his offer.

"We know how you can relieve your financial situation and do it quick. We're going to make a lot of money tomorrow evening, and we want you to be part of it. It won't even be hard work, and there's no way we'll get caught."

No way we'll get caught. No way we'll get caught. The words seemed to echo in Jonathan's head. Everything in him told him he needed to get away. Omar sat on the same sofa where Jonathan had experienced the presence of God just a few hours ago. It seemed like days and it seemed like just a few minutes all at the same time. Jonathan wanted friends. He wanted to have a good time. He wanted to drink and laugh and get high. He *didn't* want to wake up in the morning and find himself tracing the cracks in the tiles of the jail floor with his toes.

He could almost hear the same dark voice from before saying, "You know you want it. Take some. There's nothing wrong with it. These are your friends. This is good for you."

Jonathan felt the full weight of the offer. He could almost taste the beer and feel the high that would come from the drugs. Then he made a connection that changed everything. The same voice that seemed to be saying, "This is good for you," and the voice from last night that seemed to say, "God doesn't want you" were the same voice. And both were lies.

He knew these things weren't good for him because they had caused him to lose relationships. They had caused him to spend time in jail. Even if the items on the table were free, the cost of using them was too high.

Omar sat on the sofa and offered him beer, drugs and an obviously illegal opportunity to get money. On that same sofa, Jonathan had heard God offer him forgiveness and a new life. All of these thoughts ran through Jonathan's mind in just fractions of a second. Samson, Edgar, and Omar thought they'd brought Jonathan a solution and a good choice. They smiled and their eyes glowed with excitement. In their minds, they had the perfect solution for Jonathan. He just needed to make the right choice. They didn't know that Jonathan had already made his decision.

He sat on the edge of a chair and looked at these men with whom he had spent so much time. He tried to be gentle with his tone and he carefully chose his words. Still, he knew they would *not* like his answer.

"Guys, I really miss hanging out with you. But I'm sorry. I can't let drugs and alcohol be part of my life anymore. I'm not judging you for what you do, but I just can't. I still want to be friends with you, but I prayed last night and asked God to change me. I guess you could say I gave myself to Him. I can't just take my life back. I'm sorry. And I'm through doing the kinds of things that I have to worry about getting caught doing. I'm tired of jail, and I'm tired of losing people I love. I just cannot do it anymore."

"I told you he wouldn't want anything to do with us," Edgar said loudly. "He done got religion and he thinks he's better than us. You can share with him if you want to, I'm outta here!" He snatched up the drugs and slammed them back in the bag, then kicked the table over and started for the door.

"No!" Jonathan snapped. "I'm not better than anyone. I've just set myself some boundaries that I will not cross."

"Well," Omar started quietly as he slowly stood. Then he quickly grabbed Jonathan's collar and jerked him up out of his chair. Jonathan's hands grabbed Omar's wrists as Omar pulled him up nose to nose and finished, "You've crossed a boundary with us. I don't know what's poisoned you, but don't cross us again." Before he could say anything else, Samson grabbed his arm.

"Come on, Man!" Samson snarled through gritted teeth. "I want to work him over, too, but if we make enough noise for the neighbors to call the law, the whole plan is screwed!"

Omar shoved Jonathan backward into the chair as he released him. Then he turned to his companions and stepped toward the door. They totally ignored Jonathan as they cursed and roughly snatched up their belongings. They put on their shoes with snappy movements that showed their disgust and anger. In only a few seconds they were out the door. Jonathan wondered if he should try to explain more, but decided he had said all they would listen to for now. He wondered if saying something else might make them even more violent. He decided silence made the most sense. They mumbled among themselves as they walked to the car. Jonathan heard them call him a few names that he knew were not on his birth certificate.

He felt a strange mix of emptiness and victory as they sped off.

Chapter 13

Rain and DVD

Jonathan had planned to watch the DVD and work in the student workbook as soon as he got home. The unexpected visit of his friends had not only interrupted his plan, but also distracted his mind. For several minutes after they left, Jonathan meditated on what had happened. They'd been so sure that money was only the reason he was no longer hanging out with them. And they had become so angry so quickly. Would they ever understand?

Jonathan decided that friendship had not really been part of their motivation. He didn't know exactly what they'd been thinking. He found himself somewhat confused by their whole attitude.

His old friend group and his old way of life had changed so much in just the last few weeks. Jonathan found it strange that he'd contact with half of the old group in just one day. He wondered briefly what the other four were doing today.

After a few minutes, the adrenaline rush of the visit from his friends had worn off. He had seen no lightning and heard no thunder for a while, so he decided to get a shower before he started watching the video. The dust from the shop and the encounter with Omar and the others made him feel dirty. On the way up the stairs he wondered about his other friends. While he got his clothes together and ate a snack he thought about Pete and Sha'qui. He fully expected them to start dating, but he had never talked to either of them about it.

Thinking about dating made him think about Lexi. He realized they had a date, but no plan for what time or place. Since she wanted to talk about something serious, some of his favorite places to eat wouldn't work. The food might be good, but there would be no way to have a private conversation. Fast food hamburger restaurants and sports bars were not good places for that kind of date. He decided to pretend they were going on a "real date" and pick a nice place and pay for Lexi's meal. He owed her that much for not texting when he said he would. Besides that, he didn't know what her finances looked like and he didn't want to embarrass her. He also decided to call instead of text.

"Hello?" Lexi answered her phone with more of a question than a greeting.

"Hey, Lexi, this is Jonathan."

"Yeah, you were on my caller ID. What's up?" Lexi asked.

"I realized we hadn't set a time for our date," he said, with a hint of a laugh. "Would you like me to pick you up, or meet you somewhere tomorrow?"

"To be honest, I'm usually pretty hungry when I get off work. If you want to meet before I go home, we can just meet somewhere. Maybe grab a burger?"

"Okay with me," Jonathan said. "Only, let me take you to the new steak and seafood place in front of the mall. My treat."

"Oh, you don't have to do that," Lexi objected. "I was the one who wanted to talk. I should pay. Besides, that place is kind of expensive."

"I really feel bad about not texting you when I said I would, so I'll feel better if you let me pick up the tab. I like the food there, and I'm finding I have more money to spend since I'm not partying so much on the weekends. I think it'll be a better place to talk, too. We'll be able to hear one another better."

"Okay, if you really want to, I'll let you pay." She laughed, then got serious again. "The partying is something I want to ask you about, but I'll talk to you about it tomorrow. Is 6:00 good?"

"That'll be fine," he answered. "I'll see you then. Whichever one of us gets there first can go ahead and get a table. They might be busy."

"Sounds good. See you then. Bye."

Jonathan put his phone on the table next to the TV and DVD remotes and sat down. He wondered if he had made a mistake. He didn't want to take Lexi out to eat, pay for her meal, and have her try to tell him why he should not have left their group. He certainly didn't want a repeat of the kind of thing that happened tonight with the guys.

Well, he thought to himself, *it won't be the first time I paid someone to nag at me.*

He decided he'd watch some of the video before he went to bed, so he put the disk in the DVD player. The first part of the workbook told him how to use the set, so he read the first two pages and then pressed play. Before the first part began to play, his phone rang. His Uncle Steve's name displayed on the phone screen. He paused the video.

"Hello!" Jonathan said as he answered the phone.

"Hey, Boy!" Steve said with his standard greeting. "You asleep?"

"Not yet, but keep talking and I will be in a minute," Jonathan joked.

"I won't keep you, but you said you were going to clean up some in the shop tomorrow?"

"Yes, sir!" Jonathan responded. "I'm planning on going in first thing in the morning for a little while."

"That's what I was calling about. Lightning hit a transformer near the shop, and it won't have power until late tomorrow. One of my friends with the power company called me. I've already called Chelsea and told her not to come in tomorrow. I guess you can take the day off, too."

"That'll work out fine for me," Jonathan assured him. "I just got a DVD from Jimmy that I want to watch and work on, so I can do that tomorrow during the day. And I have a date tomorrow evening."

"A date?" Uncle Steve teased.

"Yeah, just a friend who wants to talk some, but it was a good excuse to eat a steak," Jonathan laughed. "Anyway, I can find something to do tomorrow. How're you feeling?"

"Some better, but I'm about to go to bed. I'll talk to you later."

"Okay. Bye, Uncle Steve."

"Bye, Son."

Jonathan had almost added an "I love you" to his good bye, but didn't. He really did love Uncle Steve, but they just normally didn't talk to one another that way. Uncle Steve's decision to go to bed so early had Jonathan more than a little concerned.

"God, would you please help Uncle Steve with whatever is wrong with him? Would you get him to see a doctor or something so he can be healthy? I need him." He hoped this would be good enough as a prayer to get God's attention. There seemed to be so much to this new life and praying that he didn't understand.

After taking a short bathroom break and getting something to drink, he started the video again. He had his pen ready and found a place on the arm of the sofa he could put the workbook while he wrote. Watching the video reminded him of many of the things he and Jimmy had talked about. The man in the introduction who had stopped using crack cocaine and crystal meth reminded Jonathan of himself in some ways.

Two hours later, he had reviewed Integrity, Breaches, Reputation, the CIRCLE-F Principle, Core Values, and Respect for Persons, Resources, and Authority. He smiled as he thought about how much he had learned from Jimmy in their casual conversations.

The sound of the rain and the effects of his long, full day made him sleepy earlier than usual. He decided to go to bed and start over in the morning. The next section of the video would be new material for him, and he wanted to be fresh when he started it. The video and workbook would still be there, and he'd be more alert after some sleep. One glass of milk and ten minutes later he turned the lights off and closed his eyes. The whole day replayed in his head, but the part with Omar, Edgar, and Samson seemed to be the loudest and longest.

He lay in the dark listening to the wind and rain outside. A tired body doesn't mean a tired mind. He found himself replaying the conversation with Omar, and then jumping to the date tomorrow night with Lexi. He wanted to look forward to it, and he dreaded it at the same time. He really didn't want her to try to draw him back into his old lifestyle, or try to make him feel guilty for not spending time with his old friends. He wanted some friends and a new lifestyle with a new group of people. Then his mind jumped to the video and some of the pages in the workbook. He had been surprised to see Angie in one of the sections, and he liked what she said about being "extraordinary, not just ordinary." He wanted to be that kind of person. He wondered how other people saw him.

The wind blew hard and the rain sounded a little louder, but something had changed. Somewhere in the storm of thoughts, sleep sneaked up on him. A wet morning tapped on his window and lit his room. He glanced at his clock. Eight fifteen. He got up slowly and began to plan out his lazy day while he ate some cereal. Other than his date this evening with Lexi, he had nothing on his schedule. He decided to watch the rest of the video before he got ready to go. He checked his wallet to be sure he had enough money for the evening, then sat down to finish the video.

Before he started the video, he looked back through his notes and stopped on the Core Values page. More and more he recognized an emptiness in his soul. He had such a longing for a mate and family. He revisited the thoughts about having children who would sit in his lap while he read to them. In his mind, he played with his little boy in the floor in front of the television. He heard his wife in the kitchen and smelled the meal she made for them.

"God, I really do want to be a good Daddy," he said aloud. Then, to the television, he said, "All right, Jimmy, let's get to work building a new man here."

The information in the video and the workbook he used seemed so practical. The next section for him was entitled Reliability. The video defined reliability as trustworthiness. That made sense. The next part about Objective Truth and Subjective Truth made him pause and remember the article about him in the newspaper. The definitions came first:

"Objective Truth is an accurate account of just the facts. 'This is a chair,' is an Objective Truth statement, the video said.

Subjective Truth is an accurate account of a fact or facts that includes personal interpretation or opinion. 'This is a beautiful chair,' is a Subjective Truth statement."

As Jonathan looked at the definitions in the workbook and watched to the video, he remembered the article the newspaper had printed about him. The writer had called him a hero. It went on to tell about his great work fixing the dam and how many lives may have been saved. Jonathan thought about the actual events. What he had really done was clean out a diversion ditch so the water would have somewhere to go. Then he put the dirt from that in the low places on the dam. He didn't see himself as a hero, only as a dirt-mover.

"Man on backhoe moves dirt and changes the flow of floodwater." Objective

Truth, but a very short newspaper article, Jonathan decided. That wouldn't sell very many papers.

"Hero on backhoe repairs dam and saves lives and property." Definitely Subjective Truth, and likely to sell more papers. Jonathan smiled. Then he began to see a more recent application of the information that he thought would help him when he talked to Lexi.

Jonathan has changed. This is an Objective Truth statement that everyone can see.

He thought to himself as he reasoned out the different perspectives. *I think the change is good. Jonathan has changed for the better. That makes it Subjective Truth.*

Omar thinks differently. "Jonathan's change is bad." He thinks I'm wrong, but we could both agree that I have changed.

Jonathan decided that he'd be honest with Lexi and tell her that he had changed. He'd tell her why he had changed and how he had changed. Their relationship after that would depend upon whether she agreed that his change was good.

He'd always thought of himself as honest enough. Since he started turning his life around, he'd have told you he was an honest man. He wouldn't have hesitated. Now, the video taught "honesty is the measure of how one treats truth." That made him change his opinion. He could see several times lately where he hadn't lied, but may have substituted Subjective Truth for Objective Truth when answering someone.

On at least one occasion, he hadn't answered when Uncle Steve asked him if he understood something. He didn't understand, but didn't want to admit that he hadn't been paying attention. He thought that he was honest if he just didn't lie. Now he began to understand that being silent and letting Uncle Steve believe something that wasn't true might not be lying, but it was still dishonest. *Ouch!*

Uncle Steve now took the front seat in Jonathan's thoughts. He decided to call and talk to him again, because he truly feared that Uncle Steve might be dying of cancer and not letting anyone know. Maybe he didn't even know himself, but he seemed to be sick or exhausted most of the time now. Sometimes he'd be pale and other times his face seemed flushed. Sometimes he seemed suddenly sleepy. Jonathan wondered what would happen to the company if Uncle Steve could no longer run it. Although Jonathan knew how to do his own part, Uncle Steve had at least two other crews that Jonathan never saw or talked to at all. Chelsea talked to them some, and Uncle Steve knew everything they did, but Jonathan knew almost nothing about them.

Uncle Steve didn't answer his phone. Was he sleeping? Working on something else? Jonathan decided to call later. He went and put a load of clothes in the washing machine, then called again. Still no answer. He started to call his mom and ask her if she knew anything, but he didn't want to worry her unnecessarily. He thought about going to Uncle Steve's house. He'd surely feel silly if Uncle Steve was just taking a nap. Still, if Uncle Steve couldn't get to his phone for some reason, or had passed out somewhere… Jonathan began to worry. He picked up his phone to try again, and it buzzed in his hand. Uncle Steve's name showed on the caller ID.

"Hello!" Jonathan's relief showed in his voice.

"Hey, Boy, you trying to find me?" Uncle Steve sounded out of breath, but in a good mood.

"Yeah," Jonathan replied, "I was just checking on you. You sound out of breath. Are you okay?"

"I'm fine," Uncle Steve responded. "I just left the doctor's office, and it's raining a little here, so I ran to the car. I'm a little out of shape."

"Now, if you're fine," Jonathan half-teased, "why are you at the doctor's office?" He didn't want to seem worried, so he added, "You aren't pregnant, are you?"

Uncle Steve laughed. "Too early to tell about that," he joked, "but I do have diabetes. I have to monitor my sugar for a while to see how bad it is. That's the reason I've been so tired and sleepy lately. It's really made me think about the company and my health. I want to talk to you next week about some plans and changes, but it's nothing for you to worry about. I'm going to be fine, and the company's okay."

"It's good to know that you're okay and to know what's wrong, but I'm sorry to hear about the diabetes," Jonathan's voice showed his relief. Then he added, "And it's good to hear that I won't be losing my new dance partner!"

Uncle Steve laughed. "Yeah, you get to keep her, and some extra work, too, I think. I'll tell you about all that next week. How is that integrity study going? Have you finished that video yet?"

"No, I'm still working on it," Jonathan answered. His voice showed his surprise. "What made you think about that?"

"I'm familiar with it, and there are some things in there that I want you to know. Then, I want us to talk about them. You've been changing a lot lately, and it's a good change. I think the information in that video and book will be good for you. Take it seriously, though. Meanwhile, have a good time on your date tonight."

"I will," Jonathan answered. Uncle Steve's interest in his growth and private life seemed to be growing. Or, maybe he just hadn't paid attention before. Sometimes he felt like he'd been in a fog and had just begun to come out. Had Uncle Steve always thought about him so much? He didn't know, but he sure had Uncle Steve on *his* mind now more than he ever had.

After he put his phone down, Jonathan said a quick, "Thank you, God!" prayer. He went to his back door and looked out at the rain. He felt restless and wished he could work today and get a little exercise. Since the weather wouldn't let him work outside, he did some pushups and crunches, then ran up and down the stairs a couple of times. He decided to put his clothes in the dryer and eat an early lunch before continuing with the video and workbook. Even if the electricity went out later, he wanted to be ready for his date. It might be wise to go ahead and shower and shave, too. On the days he worked, he didn't always shave. Sometimes he skipped shaving on his day off, too, but tonight he wanted to look presentable. Somehow he felt that tonight would mark some changes in his life, although he didn't know what or how.

He'd learn later that he'd been more correct than he'd ever dreamed.

Chapter 14

Unfolding Future

Jonathan finished eating lunch and taking a shower well before noon. He went back to start on the video and workbook again. Uncle Steve's encouraging words helped motivate him. He found himself getting curious about Uncle Steve's wanting to talk. Was he thinking about selling the company? Would they be getting more work? Did Uncle Steve want him to start working with one of the other crews? Would he be getting a raise? He'd know next week, but today he couldn't help being curious and wondering about it.

He couldn't get his date tonight out of his mind, either. Many times in the past he'd been excited about dates, but never nervous like he felt about this one. He almost felt afraid. He didn't know whether Lexi would want to criticize his life-change decision or if she had something else on her mind. He didn't know whether he'd be happy, angry, or disappointed after the date. Not knowing what Lexi was thinking had him puzzled. He wondered if they would even be friends after tonight.

As he sat down on the sofa to watch the video again, he vividly remembered last night. He could almost feel Omar's grip on his shirt and the tension that suddenly had exploded between them. In a way he couldn't explain, he felt dirty after the encounter.

I hope I don't feel like this after I talk with Lexi tonight, he thought to himself. *I'm ready for something positive to happen. Maybe she doesn't want to talk about me at all and it can just be a friendly evening.*

For a very brief moment he missed Katie. He started to wonder what their lives might've been like now if they had stayed together. Then he made himself stop. Revisiting those memories wouldn't help anything. He knew he needed to be looking forward instead of backward. Katie wouldn't be in his future. He needed to focus on today, and today he had a video to watch, a workbook to complete, and a date to keep. The clock on his phone showed he still had over six hours before he had to meet Lexi.

The next section in the video dealt with "Restraint: the act of setting and keeping boundaries." For the first time since he began the video, he felt good about what he already knew. Last night, he had kept the boundaries he'd already set for himself. He had refused the beer and drugs, so he didn't fall back into his old habits. He had made his decision clear to his old friends, and to himself. He had set and kept a good boundary.

Another part of the section also focused on setting goals and treating them as boundaries. He could see where he'd already begun to set goals for himself when he thought about his future family. In many areas, he had already been working on this cornerstone of his integrity.

As he wrote in his workbook, he started thinking about Max, a friend from his childhood. Max and his sister, Anna, had grown up not far from Jonathan. While Jonathan chose to settle for quick fun and parties in his late teen years, Max had chosen to study hard and go to college. Now, he helped with the family business and had recently become vice president. At only 25, his ability to set and keep goals had helped him succeed. For a moment Jonathan envied Max. He had a wife, a college degree, and a future, and he seemed to be very happy with the decisions he had made. Max had always set goals. Jonathan had not.

Okay, Jonathan thought, *I can't have Max's life, but I can have mine. I am a person of value and worthy of respect. That means that I'm also worthy of a future. It's a fact that I've been lazy and haven't set good boundaries and goals. I know that it's my responsibility to set them. So,* he thought, looking at his workbook, *since Responsibility is the next section, it looks like I'm on track.*

Before he started the next session, he set the alarm on his phone for 5:00. Then he double checked to be sure he set it for p.m. That would give him plenty of time to get ready to meet Lexi. Setting the alarm would keep him from continually watching the clock and reminding himself about the date. He still felt butterflies in his stomach when he thought about it. He honestly didn't know whether he felt more excitement or fear. He felt excitement at the idea of spending time with someone and not having to eat alone again. He hoped they would have some good conversation. At the same time, he feared that Lexi would try to pressure him to make compromises he didn't want to make.

He tried to get the fear and dread out of his mind by turning his focus to the video. In just a few minutes he'd finished the session on Responsibility and watched the video for the session on Accountability. He'd already talked about accountability with Jimmy and Angie earlier. He decided that he'd ask them, his mom, and Uncle Steve to be his accountability partners and help keep him on track. The workbook had sections where they could sign a commitment to be his partners. His responsibility would be to ask them to hold him accountable in a certain area, or certain areas, of his life. The old Jonathan would've put the decision off until later. The new Jonathan picked up his phone to call Jimmy and Angie now.

Jimmy answered on the first ring. "Hello, there!" his lively voice seemed to bounce through Jonathan's phone.

"Hello, Jimmy," Jonathan answered with equal brightness. "Are you busy today?"

"Busy watching the rain and drinking coffee," Jimmy answered. "Are you working today?"

"No, Sir," Jonathan replied. "I'm actually watching the video and working on my book. I called to ask you to be one of my accountability partners and keep me on track."

"I would be honored," Jimmy started, "but you'll have to stay in touch for me to do that. I won't be able to track you down."

"I plan on coming by the office regularly, so that won't be a problem," Jonathan said with a smile. "I'm also planning to ask Angie if she will help me."

"Are you going to call her later? She's sitting right here. I can put you on speaker phone if you want."

"That would be great," Jonathan agreed. Then, after a brief pause, he said, "Hello, Angie."

"Hello, Jonathan," Angie said with her usual energy. "How are you this fine, wet day?"

"I'm quacking and waddling!" Jonathan joked. "How about you?"

"I'm keeping my bones warm with coffee and bill paying," Angie replied. "Are you working in all this?"

"No, I'm at home. I'm actually watching the DVD and working in my student book today. That's what I was calling for," Jonathan said. "I wanted to ask you if you would be one of my accountability partners. Specifically, I want you to remind me to be the kind of son that my mom can be proud of."

"I think that's a wonderful goal," Angie answered energetically. "I'd be glad to do that for you!"

Jonathan heard their office phone ringing in the background, and it reminded him that they were working. "I won't hold you up. I'll talk to both of you about it later," he said.

Jimmy answered him. "I just took the phone off speaker and Angie went to answer the other phone. Are you working on more of the video today?"

"Yes, sir," Jonathan answered. "I plan to finish it before I meet with a friend this evening. I'm enjoying it, but, to be honest, I'm getting tired of being indoors all day!"

"Don't burn yourself out working on it," Jimmy said seriously. "Take your time. The next couple of parts are pretty intense."

"Thank you, sir," Jonathan assured him. "I will. Would it be okay if I come there for a few hours Monday? I'd like to talk to you about some of this, and maybe work on it there if I won't be in the way."

"That'll be fine," Jimmy answered. "I'll look forward to seeing you."

"I'll see you then." Jonathan signed off and put his phone back on the sofa.

The rain fell harder and the wind blew louder as Jonathan settled in for the next session. The lights went off, then back on, and his television went dark. The DVD player also blinked and reset. He decided to take a break, move around some, and look outside. The clouds seemed to be racing one another, and the pine trees on the far side of the parking lot were obviously having a dancing contest. He opened the door to look outside and immediately stepped back and closed it. Too much rain and wind. It also felt much cooler.

Cookies and a cup of hot apple cider would be a good break. Taking a few minutes to be sure the power would stay on seemed like a good reason for a break, too. He put a cup of apple cider in the microwave and went up and down the stairs quickly to get some exercise while it heated. He got his cookies and his cup of cider and returned to the sofa. For the first time he noticed the title of the next session: Forgiveness.

When he started the video, he halfway expected a lecture on the need to forgive. He found much more. Most of the session focused on one man's personal story of pain, betrayal, and the struggle with a choice between murder and forgiveness. Jonathan found himself captivated by the man's true story. The man's decision to forgive instead of trying to "get even" held Jonathan's attention more than any of the other parts of the video had. To be sure he really understood the whole story, Jonathan watched the session again. Then, he replayed the events in his mind.

Someone hurt, killed, or injured some member of the man's family. The man, JD, decided he must kill the guilty person to get even. He planned to kill the guilty person on the courthouse steps. Then, something in JD's core values made him think about what he had planned. He decided to forgive, not murder, the man.

Jonathan paused to organize his thoughts. Forgiveness means to "remove the guilt and give up the right to 'even the score'." It didn't mean that the event or action suddenly became acceptable. It didn't mean that the trust or the original relationship had been restored. It meant that the injured person refused to be anchored to one event for the rest of his life.

One statement from the video echoed in Jonathan's mind as he read the same words in the workbook: "If you don't allow yourself to forgive, all you're going to do is allow yourself to be eaten on the inside by rage and anger." Jonathan knew what it meant to be eaten by rage and anger. He'd felt that way most of his adult life. Sometimes, he'd used alcohol as an escape.

The sections in the workbook asked questions to help the student work through some areas of forgiveness. They focused on forgiving others, forgiving yourself, and asking those you have hurt for forgiveness. The first people Jonathan thought about forgiving were Omar, Edgar, and Samson. He knew they would never ask for forgiveness, so it would take some extra effort on his part. He might have to add Lexi after tonight, but he quickly put that thought on hold.

His words and attitude towards Katie put her on the top of the list of people he needed to ask for forgiveness. He found that he also needed to forgive himself for that. This process of forgiveness wouldn't be finished this afternoon. He began to wonder if some of the anger he seemed to always feel inside could be rooted in some unforgiven incident or relationship.

Suddenly, a rockslide of memories and emotions from his childhood, all focused on his father, came rumbling through his mind. He remembered his father cursing him and being too drunk to remember it later. He could still feel the back of his father's hand slapping his mouth when he asked for something else to eat. In later years, his father became less violent, but more emotionally distant. He focused on working just enough to buy his next bottle. He had no room in his alcoholic life for his family.

Memories from his childhood flooded Jonathan's mind, and he had to say aloud, "Dad, I forgive you for that," many times. He felt numb and overwhelmed. The memories swarmed and he began to try to sort through his emotions. In the back of his mind, he remembered his date for tonight and felt the urge to get ready. Without thinking, he started up the stairs to the bathroom.

His heart felt raw and his mind seemed to swim as he adjusted the water and got into the shower. He just stood there as he cried and yelled at his father while struggling with the memories. He prayed and cried some more as he began to work through years of poisonous memories that had kept him angry in the depths of his heart. Finally, he composed himself enough to realize that he had just showered a couple of hours ago.

Jonathan felt emotionally drained. He turned off the water and stepped out of the shower. Part of him wanted to talk to his father and tell him how much damage he had done. He wanted to remind his father of all the wrong things he had done. He knew he needed to forgive his father, and he was trying, but at the same time he wanted his father to feel the pain he had felt. Then he looked at the mirror and his heart dropped. The heat from the shower had fogged up the mirror so much that he couldn't see his reflection. But the fog that concealed his reflection revealed a message and a lesson.

A few months ago, a construction crew dug up the water supply line and the water had been turned off at Katie's apartment. She had taken a shower here. She had written "I love you" on one side of the mirror, and "always, Katie" just under it with her finger. The fingerprints kept the mirror from fogging where she touched it. The invisible message could only be read when the mirror fogged up like it did now.

A bitter reality stared Jonathan in the face. He felt the hurt of the mistakes and breaches of his father. They hurt him and he couldn't forget them. Here, on the mirror, he saw a vivid reminder of his own mistakes and breaches that had hurt someone else. He couldn't forget *them* either. He had made mistakes. With all his heart he wanted forgiveness, although he couldn't say he deserved it.

In a moment of clarity in a steamy bathroom Jonathan realized that he must offer forgiveness if he wanted to be forgiven. He felt the room spin as the nuggets of wisdom exploded in his head. He must be willing to forgive his father as honestly and completely as he wanted Katie to forgive him. Since he wanted his mom to forgive him for hurting her, he had to forgive Omar for hurting him. On top of all of this, Jonathan had to forgive Jonathan.

One thing is very clear to me, Jonathan thought to himself. *I may finish the book and video today, but I won't finish all the work today. I may be working on parts of this for the rest of my life.*

He decided to go ahead and get dressed so he'd be completely ready for tonight. Since he had already taken two showers today, he figured he wouldn't need another one in the next two hours. He picked the dark blue polo shirt and khakis for tonight. While he dressed and then went downstairs, he thought about forgiveness.

He found the workbook and his pen both on the floor when he went back downstairs. He'd never heard them fall when he left them. The video still waited for him at the end of his last session. He picked up the workbook and found the last part he had completed. Several pages in the workbook had blanks for him to answer questions or to write the names of people he needed to forgive. Some of the pages dealt with things he felt like he had just washed down the drain. It didn't take long to write down the information, but it would take many days to do what he needed to do. One of the sections had a paragraph that Jonathan thought must have been written just for him.

"Sometimes we have to draw boundaries in relationships to protect ourselves. This may even mean breaking off a relationship with someone. That is okay – even healthy."

He decided Ashleigh needed to read that, too. In fact, he decided to send her a copy of the book and DVD when she could receive mail in rehab. He planned talk to Jimmy about that when he saw him again.

After the section on forgiveness, he found a short session on Humility. Many of the things the video and book said were things he had just realized on his own in the last hour. "Humility is realizing that you are not perfect." Realizing you're not perfect helps you forgive others. He'd just come face to face with that reality in the bathroom upstairs. One broken heart plus one foggy mirror equaled one clear and vivid lesson.

With an hour and a half to spend before he had to leave, Jonathan decided he'd try to finish the workbook today. He had no doubt that he'd revisit the material several times in the next few days. He wondered how he would ever put into practice all he had learned. He'd need some kind of plan.

Discipline came next in the book. To Jonathan's surprise, he found that the author of the material had already thought about the need for a written plan. The old adage, "Practice makes perfect," seemed to be the main message here. The author clearly stated that it is possible something perfectly wrong, so you need to practice success. This section flowed right into the Fortification Plan in the next session where students could write out their plans for success.

Part of the last session also dealt with addiction, and Jonathan could see where Jimmy got his definition. When he and Jimmy had talked about core values, Jimmy had told him, "Any behavior that you repeat until it begins to replace or destroy one or more of your core values is an addiction." He could clearly see that Jimmy had been informally teaching him this material all along. Jonathan knew that it would take a long time before he had fully changed his life. He hoped Jimmy would continue to help him.

When Jonathan had finished about half of the Fortification Plan, his phone alarm sounded. He had one hour before he and Lexi were to meet. Since he was already ready to go, he wanted to work on his Fortification Plan for a few more minutes. He reached for his phone to turn the alarm off and noticed that he had some text messages. The time tag on each of them indicated they had come in while he was in the shower.

Omar's was first, and said, *"You are really missing out permanently, LOSER!"* Jonathan decided to ignore it completely.

Lexi's was second, *"I may be about 10 minutes late. Sorry!"*

He responded quickly, *"That will be fine. I was away from my phone. Sorry for the late response."*

Jonathan finished his workbook and put on his shoes. Parts of the Fortification Plan might need to be revised in a couple of hours, depending upon how his conversation with Lexi went. All day, he had been excited and a little nervous about the date. Right now, he didn't feel either of those nearly as much as he felt hunger. He whistled as he hurried through the light rain to his truck. The drive to the restaurant seemed short, and he saw very few cars on the road. Maybe the weather had kept everyone inside.

He thought he saw Lexi's car as he parked and started for the door. Now, the butterflies in his stomach started again.

Chapter 15

Date Surprises

"Memory movies" played in Jonathan's head as he walked across the parking lot at the *Beef and Reef* steakhouse. He saw himself and Katie on one of their dates here. They held hands and walked across the parking lot. They talked about their future. He smiled at the happy scenes as he walked through the space where they had parked that night.

In another movie, he watched Lexi sitting with his other friends at the picnic table at Aunt Jo's. He remembered the looks of anger and disbelief as he told them about his life change. Then, his heart pounded as he thought about the rejection and anger in the eyes of the guys in his living room. Would Lexi continue the pressure and criticism? His smile disappeared.

For a brief moment, he almost decided not to go in and face Lexi. Still, there had always been something a little different about her. Maybe she'd be different. *At least,* he thought, *maybe she won't be so mean about it.*

When Jonathan walked in the door, he saw a familiar face. Kayla's smile greeted him from across the dining room. He knew that she worked at Aunt Jo's, but he had no idea that she also worked here. From what he knew about her and her work at Aunt Jo's, he figured she'd make good tips here. He thought about asking the hostess to seat him in Kayla's area, but he saw that Lexi already had a booth on the back wall. Walking across the dining room, he passed the table where he and Katie had sat on their last date here. The plates and drinks from the last two people who ate there still sat on the table. A small tip waited for the server to pick it up.

Lexi seemed almost shy when he arrived at the table. He sat facing her and briefly looked around the room.

"Hey," he said, "I ran a little later than I thought."

She smiled. "And I actually got off work a little earlier than I expected."

Before any other conversation started, Kayla appeared at the table. "Hello, I'm Kayla and I will be serving you tonight. Will this be together or separate?"

Jonathan noted the questions in Kayla's eyes. As their server, she asked how many checks to bring to the table tonight. As his "little sister from the diner" she wanted to know if Lexi was his girlfriend.

"Just one," Jonathan answered as he looked in Kayla's eyes and smiled, "I'm buying dinner for my friend tonight."

"Okay," Kayla continued, "would you like to go ahead and order drinks or an appetizer now?"

Decision time. He fully expected Lexi to order wine with her meal. What would he order? He had decided not to drink any alcohol for a while since he and Jimmy had talked about addictions. Jonathan had been thinking all day about the steak and sweet potato he wanted to order, but he hadn't thought about the drinks. Four months ago, he would've already ordered a beer. Now, he wondered if he should order any alcohol at all. Could he handle alcohol? Would a small glass be okay? What would Lexi's response be? The short, two-second pause while all these questions ran through his mind seemed to be much longer to him. Before he could run through all the possible answers and make a decision, Kayla rescued him.

"If you want your usual," she began, smiling and looking at Jonathan, "I can get that for you. If you want something from the bar, I can take your order and someone else will bring it to you."

Jonathan decided to let Lexi order first. He motioned to her, and she quickly answered, "I'll have what you're having."

He hadn't expected that response, and he hadn't come prepared to make decisions. In the short, awkward pause that followed, Kayla patiently waited and smiled. Finally, she prompted him a little.

"May I suggest," she started as she pointed to an item on the menu, "the chip and dip appetizer?"

Jonathan looked at Lexi, who smiled and nodded without looking at the menu. Then he nodded at Kayla.

"Okay," she said, "that's two teas and one chip and dip. Is light ice okay for the tea?" She looked quickly at Lexi to double check the drink order. After Lexi nodded, Kayla continued, "I'll be right back." She smiled and disappeared toward the kitchen.

"You look a little distracted. Are you tired?" Lexi asked.

"A little, I guess," Jonathan answered. "I've been working on some things at home all day today, and maybe I'm a little brain-weary. Being trapped in my living room all day always makes me foggy. I like being active."

"I fully understand. This weather has me feeling a little sluggish, too." Then, she paused for a few seconds. "What are we ordering for dinner?" Lexi asked, as if they ate together every day.

"I'm thinking about the number four sirloin with a sweet potato and salad. You can get whatever you want. I've got it," he said, giving her a quick smile.

"I'll have what you're having," she stated. Then she added, "It really sounds good."

Kayla returned with their drinks and appetizer, took their order, and moved on again. Jonathan's eyes followed her for a moment as she stopped at another table briefly, then went to the kitchen. She looked pretty tonight, and he wondered if she'd gotten a haircut or something.

"Do you come here often?" Lexi asked. "She seems to know you pretty well."

"No, I've been here some, but I've never seen her here before," Jonathan laughed. "She knows me from Aunt Jo's. When I first met her there, I thought she had a crush on me, but then I realized she's just really good at her job. She's like everybody's little sister."

"I thought she looked familiar!" Lexi said. "This is the first time I've been here, but I thought I knew her. She looks different with the uniform and her hair fixed this way. She's the one who got my take-out order together for work the day I told you I wanted to talk."

"The last couple of times I've seen you, it's been at Aunt Jo's," Jonathan said.

"That's part of what I want to talk to you about," Lexi started, "you know, about that last time we actually talked there. None of us had seen you for a while; then we saw you at Aunt Jo's. When you came to talk at the picnic table, I didn't like how that turned out."

Jonathan braced himself. *Uh oh,* he thought. He decided not to be defensive or try to explain. He'd just let her talk.

"Jonathan, we've never talked much. I mean, never *really* talked about serious things. I feel like I need to share something with you. I never had a solid and functional family. I love my family, but there is no way you could call any of it stable. When I left home and moved out on my own, I got very lonely. Then I started hanging out with you guys. It was kind of a family substitute, if you know what I mean."

Here we go, Jonathan thought. *She's going to talk about our group being her family and I'm leaving them. After what happened with Omar, Edgar and Samson, though, I don't think things can ever be the way they were.*

"I've been in the group totally for the family feeling," she continued. "Since our focus was the drugs and drinks, I always thought the rest of my life would be in that group doing those things. When you and Katie got together, I thought you two would get married and we'd still be doing the same things. I never thought about any of us not being there anymore. It never occurred to me that any or all of us might, one day, leave. My whole world has been totally focused on our weekends."

Kayla brought their food and interrupted Lexi for a minute. She refilled Jonathan's tea and asked if they needed anything else. While they paused for Kayla to place their food on the table, Jonathan had put his hands on the table. Kayla smiled and went to the next table. When Kayla had left, he interrupted the flow of the conversation with an unexpected request.

"Lexi, I have been trying to get in a habit of praying before I eat. Do you mind?" he asked.

Lexi's surprise showed in her smile. She said, "I don't mind at all. In fact, I'd like that."

"God, thank you for this food and the time that we are spending together. Amen." Jonathan looked at Lexi and explained, "I'm new at this praying thing, so, I hope I don't sound too, um, too awkward."

"It was fine," Lexi said. Something about her seemed to change, to soften some. They both started to eat.

"Getting back to what you were saying about always being together as a party family: I was that same way," Jonathan confessed. "We had some fun, but I finally realized I had to make a change."

"I know. When you told us that day that you were changing, everyone thought you were crazy and that you'd be back. I think the guys even had a bet on how long it would take. They all thought you should change your mind and come back. But you didn't." Lexi paused.

"I couldn't," Jonathan added. "It's hard to explain, but I had to start thinking about what's really important to me. I know everyone thought I was a traitor, and I'm sorry if you felt abandoned, but –"

"No!" Lexi interrupted. "When you left, I didn't want you to come back in, I wanted to follow you out." She paused and put down her fork. "For the first time in my adult life, I began to see that there could be a different future. You didn't look like a traitor to me. You looked like hope."

Jonathan stopped in mid-chew. Probably nothing Lexi could have said would've surprised him more. She had no intention of trying to get him back to his old lifestyle. If he heard what he thought he heard, she wanted to follow him out.

"What I really want to know," she continued, "and the reason I wanted to talk to you, is this. If it's not too personal and you don't mind telling me, how did you change, and why did you change, and do you think it would work for me?" Lexi's questions seemed to come like a train, with each one linked to the one before it.

Jonathan started to chew again. He managed a muffled, "Wow!" He finally swallowed and said, "That's not what I expected you to want to talk about at all, but I don't mind telling you if I can put it in words."

They ate in silence for a few minutes while Jonathan gathered his thoughts. How could he explain it all? Lexi spoke next.

"I'm sorry. I didn't mean to put you on the spot," she said softly. "What I meant was, I see major changes in you. You seem to be getting more solid and complete. You seem to be liking the changes, but I know they can't be easy. Still, you're doing it. I see something in you that I like," her voice trailed off to silence as she finished with, "and I want it for myself." She turned her focus to her plate.

"I'm not sure I know exactly how to answer," Jonathan replied. "But the short answer is that I've started working on my personal integrity and I've asked God to help me. I'm meeting with Jimmy Betts and he's kind of guiding me."

Lexi had finished eating, and she slid her plate back. She had finished the meal, but Jonathan could see that she still had a hunger for what he had to say.

"I worked last night and all day today on a video and workbook called *Castles of Character*. It's a way of working on my personal integrity. I got it from Jimmy. It's divided into units where you watch the video and then fill in the workbook. The introduction says it's designed to be used by small groups or by individuals. If you want, I could get you one." Jonathan looked into Lexi's eyes, trying to measure her response.

"I don't know," she answered cautiously.

"It's not a religious thing, not a Bible study or anything. It could be, but I meant that there's no preacher kind of stuff in it," he said.

"I'm not sure. I know, well, I can try." She stumbled over the words.

"If you want," Jonathan offered, "we could go through it together. I'm going to do it again anyway, and we could watch the video and talk about it together."

Lexi perked up and began to glow. "If you want, we could watch it at my place, and I could make something to eat or we could order a pizza."

Jonathan saw an answer to some of his lonely evenings, and an opportunity to help a friend, all rolled up in an accountability partner. He quickly agreed. "Sounds great."

Kayla came back to bring the check and see if they needed refills or dessert. Jonathan noticed that she really did look different. Lexi had been right; she'd done something with her hair and make-up.

"You sure are pretty tonight, Kayla. Did you do something different with your hair?" he asked.

"Thank you! I did get it trimmed and styled," Kayla beamed. "Thank you for noticing!"

"You're welcome," Jonathan said. He had already looked at the check, and handed it with some money back to Kayla. "I don't need change. Thanks. You've been great, as always."

Lexi watched Kayla's eyes and Jonathan's reaction as Kayla took the money and the check. Kayla seemed to appreciate the comment about her hair more than the tip, which had been quite generous. Lexi focused on Jonathan's eyes for a moment as he looked at Kayla. She could tell that he had no romantic interest or bad intentions toward Kayla. He just genuinely wanted her to feel good about herself. Lexi had never noticed that quality in Jonathan before. Had it always been there, or had he changed that much? She didn't know.

Sirens and lights brought everyone's attention to the front of the restaurant. Two law enforcement officers in different parts of the restaurant quickly stood and hurried to the front door. Blue lights seemed to light up the all the windows and doors. Jonathan saw three police cars and two Emergency Response vans speed past.

"Looks like there might have been a bad wreck," Lexi said. "I hope no one was hurt."

"Whatever it's, it's big," Jonathan replied.

A few people stood and went to the front of the restaurant to see what was going on outside. Some actually left. Gradually, the people at their tables and booths returned to their private conversations. Still, they occasionally paused to look toward the front door. Jonathan and Lexi rose to leave, since they were finished and had already paid. From the front door, they could see blue and red lights clustered near the Corner Mart on the other end of the block, across the street from the mall.

When they got to Lexi's car, they stood for a minute and watched the lights. Suddenly, both their phones began to ring at the same time. They both instinctively answered, without even looking to see who called. To Jonathan's great surprise, he heard Chelsea's voice.

"Mom, I need you to come get me," she said, obviously panicked. "I'm in the mall parking lot."

"Chelsea," Jonathan answered loudly to get her attention, "this is Jonathan. You called the wrong number. Are you okay?"

"Jonathan, I'm in the mall parking lot. The store where I was getting gas just got robbed, and I ran."

Jonathan had started looking for her as soon as she said something about the mall parking lot. Of course, she could be on the other side of the mall, but she sounded so desperate. He finally saw her walking, or rather, stumbling, from the direction of all the blue lights.

"I see you, and I'm coming to you," Jonathan said quickly.

"Lexi, I'll be right back," he called as he began to run toward Chelsea. It took a couple of minutes to catch her and get her to stop trying to run from him.

When he got to Chelsea, she had almost collapsed in the parking lot.

She had somehow called her mother and was trying to talk to her. She kept telling her mother, "I'm okay, but they were shooting. The girl got hit. They were shooting. The girl got hit."

Jonathan took the phone and told Chelsea's mother where to find them. It took some time to calm her down and help her understand exactly where they would be. Then he walked, half-carrying Chelsea, back to where Lexi still stood by her car, talking to someone on her cellphone.

"I'm sorry I ran off," Jonathan started, then stopped in mid-sentence.

Lexi leaned against her car, trembling and pale, holding her phone by her side. Tears streamed down her face, and she seemed unable, or unwilling, to talk. Several minutes passed with Jonathan having no idea what to do. He stood quietly, trying to keep Chelsea from passing out, and wondering what Lexi's call had been that made her so upset.

Finally, Chelsea's mother arrived. She had to hug Chelsea for a long time before Chelsea could calm down enough to talk.

"I had just finished pumping gas and put the gas cap back on," she said as she looked into her mother's eyes. "Two girls started fighting and screaming right in front of the front door of the store. I didn't know what to do, so I started to get back in my car. Then, I heard shots and both of the girls fell down. One was bleeding bad. I was scared and wanted to call you. I don't remember what happened after that until I was walking with Jonathan."

Chelsea's mother looked at Jonathan and said, "Hi, I'm Jenny, Chelsea's mom. Thank God you were here! Do you know what happened?"

"No, Ma'am," Jonathan replied. "I know less than she does. She called me first and thought she'd called you. Then I saw her in the parking lot and ran to her. When I got there, you were talking to her. That's when I talked to you on the phone. Then, I walked her back here. I guess her car is still at the store."

"I'll try to take her back there to get it. I would imagine that the police are looking for her, since her car is probably still at the gas pump. Thanks again!"

Jenny helped the trembling Chelsea into her car, and slowly drove toward the flashing lights. Jonathan said a quick, silent prayer, and turned to Lexi.

Jonathan stood quietly trying to figure out what had happened, and what to say to Lexi. She tried several times to talk to him, and each time got choked up and couldn't say anything. She waved her hand as if fanning her eyes, and mouthed, "I'm sorry."

After some time had passed, and Jonathan had no clue how long, Pete and Sha'qui walked up.

"Did she tell you what happened?" Pete asked.

"No," Jonathan answered, realizing that Pete or Sha'qui must have been the ones who called Lexi. "Chelsea, a girl who works for my uncle, said she had been pumping gas at the station on the corner. She was freaked out. She kept saying something about it getting robbed."

Pete and Sha'qui looked at one another, then at Lexi. Then they stepped closer to Jonathan and Pete said, "Man, we gotta talk."

Chapter 16

What Happened

When Jonathan had parked his car at the restaurant and went in to meet Lexi at 6:04, he had no idea where his other friends were. Pete and Sha'qui had just ordered tacos at the Mexican restaurant across the road and saw Jonathan get out of his truck. The rest of their group had totally different plans for the evening.

Omar had picked up Edgar and Samson at their apartment nine miles away at 6:05. While he waited for them, he checked to see if Jonathan had responded to the text he sent earlier. He had been angry hours before when he had texted, *"You are really missing out permanently, LOSER!"* Jonathan hadn't responded. Still mad from last night, Omar cursed and slammed his hand on the steering wheel just before Edgar and Samson jumped into the car.

"You still upset about last night?" Edgar asked. "You need to chill, man! You need a clear head tonight."

"Yeah, I know," Omar responded. "It's just, well, yeah, I know." He drove away in silence.

In another part of town, Elle stopped just long enough to let Hannah get into her car at almost the same time. Their part of the plan sounded absolutely simple. Elle and Hannah would cause a disturbance while Omar, Edgar, and Samson picked up some easy money. No one would get caught and they would be in and out it in about two minutes.

Things do not always go as planned.

When Elle and Hannah arrived at the Corner Mart convenience

147

store, they drove around the block and chose their escape plan before they parked. The store did a huge amount of business because of its location. It occupied one corner of a major four-way intersection; the mall, a bank, and a drug store occupied the other three. Elle backed into a parking space facing the highway so they could leave quickly. She made sure no one could park in front of her so she had a clear path for their escape. Then they got out and headed for their spot just outside the store entrance. When they got to their places in front of the door, they waited for their signal.

Omar, Edgar, and Samson chose a spot behind the Corner Mart in an empty section of a parking lot next door. They wanted a fast route in and out the back door of the store for a quick escape. The darkness of the parking lot would give them some cover. They had wanted Jonathan to drive so the car could be ready for them when they returned. It made Omar angry every time he thought about Jonathan turning them down. They planned to hide at Pete's place afterward and use him as an alibi. Also, since he owned property, he might be able to bail them out if they were caught. None of them thought they could get caught, but *if* they did, they wanted him to be able to help. Somehow, they never got around to letting Pete in on that part of the plan, though.

If they had parked any closer, they might have been blocked in by traffic. They parked their car and slipped over the guardrail and down the hill behind the Corner Mart's trash dumpster. It hid them from passing traffic in front of the store. They would need their fastest but most silent moves tonight. If everything went well, no one would even know the store had been robbed until much later.

The trash truck had just emptied the dumpster earlier that day, and the wet ground smelled like garbage. Edgar sneaked quickly across the narrow driveway that separated the dumpster from the back door. *Good thing this part is paved,* he thought. *These are new shoes.* His running shoes made no sound. In just a few seconds, he opened the door and signaled Omar and Samson.

Samson sent a one-word text to Elle, *"Go,"* then put his phone in his pocket. He and Omar quickly crossed the driveway and slipped passed Edgar and into the store. Within just a few seconds, they heard two women screaming and fighting in front of the store. Hannah and Elle had begun the distraction. As quickly and quietly as they could, the three men crept through the small hallway, across the stockroom and into the office. Samson went straight to the safe and began to open it using a key Edgar had stolen and given him. Omar and Edgar continued without a sound toward a door with a small window in it. It should be the door that opened behind the counter where the cash register would be waiting. They carefully peeped through the small window and watched the attendant as he went to check on the fighting women.

With one quick, silent motion, they opened the door and ducked down to hide behind the counter as they sneaked to the cash register. Suddenly, they found a problem with their plan. An attendant stood behind the register and almost out of sight. Two attendants were working tonight! They hadn't expected this. Edgar's information said only one would be working. No one will ever know who got the biggest surprise: the attendant, Omar, or Edgar. All three fully believed that their hearts stopped for a second.

As the attendant reached for something under the counter, Omar and Edgar panicked and reached for their handguns. Neither of them knew that the other had one, but both drew and fired shots at the attendant. The sounds of their own shots startled both Omar and Edgar so much that they panicked. They forgot to aim, and just fired.

When the shots exploded in the small store, customers screamed and ran. One of the shots hit the cash register, making sparks fly. Four other shots went wild toward the front of the store. The windows and glass door at the entrance of the store seemed to explode. Large holes appeared where the safety glass shattered and rained down into sparkling puddles on the floor and sidewalk. The attendant they aimed at immediately went to the floor. Both thought they had killed him. The attendant who had gone to check on the girls seemed to disappear.

Omar and Edgar spun around to exit through the door where they had entered. Samson, trying to come to their rescue, hit the door at the same time. For a moment, they all pushed the door from different directions and it refused to move. The sounds of screams and falling store items filled the air. Customers were jumping through the broken windows and running for their cars. Some hid behind shelves in the store. Omar and Edgar realized that Samson blocked their exit and began to yell at him. He seemed to be frozen, looking through the window in the door toward the front of the store. They realized that he wouldn't move, so they both spun around to run out the front of the store. Then, they both became statues.

Two scenes of horror unfolded as they turned around. The attendant they thought they had killed was huddled under the counter with a cell phone. Looking over him and out in front of the store, they saw two women lying in pools of blood. Elle had a hole in her chest and lay motionless on the concrete. A few feet away, Hannah had her hands to her face and seemed to be having seizures.

The shots that Omar and Edgar had fired had missed the intended target and hit their friends instead. One bullet had literally broken Elle's heart. She died before she hit the ground. The bullet that found Hannah had spared her life but stolen her beauty. Although it hit no bone, it gouged out the flesh of her left cheek just below the cheekbone. She would live, but life as she had known it would be no more.

City police, county sheriff's officers, and the state police all convened on the Corner Mart in just a matter of a few minutes. Ambulance and rescue units also sped to the scene. Some of the store's customers had jumped into their cars and sped off when the shooting started. Others, including Chelsea, fled the scene on foot and left their cars and trucks. Some still hid in the store. Other than Hannah and Elle, no one else had any gunshot injuries. Several had bruises. Two people needed stitches for cuts from the broken glass. One car had a bullet hole in it.

Memories of the two women lying on the ground would haunt all three of their partners in crime for the rest of their lives. Omar, Edgar, and Samson became so numbed with shock that the officers who responded to the 911 call had no problem with the arrest. The men readily surrendered and told the officers what had happened while many of the customers listened. The EMTs who responded took Hannah to a hospital, where they took her straight into surgery. She would always have a scar for a reminder. The EMTs had to leave Elle for the coroner.

The plan had called for the friends to be in and out in two minutes, with plenty of money and no chance of getting caught. Only the two-minute part actually worked. Two minutes after Elle had received the text from Samson, a bullet from one of her friends took her life. Everyone at the Corner Mart that night had their lives changed by the actions of those five friends. Four friends lived, but all five closed chapters in their lives.

Sha'qui's cousin, Dori, had been pumping gas just a few feet from Chelsea when the shooting started. She heard one of the bullets hit her car and immediately dropped to the ground. For what seemed like hours she waited for a bullet to hit her. She buried her face in her hands and remained as motionless as she could until the shooting stopped. Finally, she looked around and saw the broken glass and clutter. Then she saw Elle and Hannah lying on the ground. At first she thought it had been a drive-by shooting, then she saw Omar and Edgar inside holding guns and realized what had happened. She slowly got up, but found herself too weak to walk.

Some of the other customers were calling 911. Some were hiding and crying. Some, like Chelsea, had simply run off. Three cars were still running, but had no drivers and the doors were open.

Dori found herself blocked in by police cars and couldn't leave. She had no idea how long it had been since the shooting started. She looked around and recognized Omar and the other two men as Sha'qui's friends. Dori instinctively called Sha'qui to see if she had been part of the robbery and shooting; and to see if she had been hurt.

Pete and Sha'qui had been having dinner together at the Cancun Dunes Mexican Restaurant. The server had just cleared the plates from their meal and they were finishing their drinks. They had been watching the flashing lights and wondering what could have happened. Just before they had stood to leave, Sha'qui's phone rang.

Dori talked so loudly that Pete could hear everything she said. "Sha'qui, are you okay?" she almost screamed.

"Yes," Sha'qui answered. "What's wrong?" She looked at Pete, puzzled.

"Were you with them? Are you here? Where are you?" Dori sounded almost hysterical.

"I'm at Cancun Dunes eating tacos with Pete, Dori. Am I with who? What're you talking about?" Sha'qui asked as she leaned forward in her seat. Her eyes widened and she wrinkled her forehead.

Dori answered excitedly, "With Omar and them others that tried to hold up the Corner Mart and did the shooting. They shot out the windows of the store, shot my car, killed that girl. Maybe killed both of those girls. No—one is still alive. I think. She's shot in the face or head. Let me look…There's them other two. I think their names are Edgar and Samson.

They talking to the police. Hold on a second," she said as she paused and listened. She stood close enough for Sha'qui to hear Omar's voice.

Sha'qui, too shocked to reply, looked at Pete. He could hear Dori and found himself without words, too. Both knew that Omar had asked Pete to do something with them, and wondered if this could have been it.

"Oh, my God, Sha'qui," Dori started in a low voice, then stopped. "Sha'qui!" she said, louder. Then, "Sha'qui!" This time she screamed.

"What?" Sha'qui asked as she and Pete both stood and started for the door.

"Sha'qui, the dead girl is Elle!" Dori said loudly and began to cry.

The room went dark for Sha'qui, and her knees grew so weak that she almost fell. Pete caught her and they continued toward the exit and the car while Dori gave a few more details. When she leaned against the car, she realized that Dori had hung up. Or she had hung up on Dori. She couldn't remember which.

"We can't get to them at the Corner Mart because of the police, but we need to go tell Lexi and Jonathan, if they don't already know," Sha'qui said and started to punch in Lexi's number.

"I know," Pete said, "I see them across the road walking toward their cars. We're going to them now. Tell them not to leave."

As Pete backed out of the parking space, he and Sha'qui could still see Jonathan and Lexi. They watched as both Jonathan and Lexi reached for their phones at the same time. Sha'qui tried to collect herself as Lexi answered.

"Lexi, this is Sha'qui," she started. "I have to tell you something." Her voice quivered and she fell silent.

Pete decided not to try to simply cross the busy highway because of all the traffic. He decided to turn right, go to the next traffic light, U-turn and come back. All of the commotion with the police cars and Emergency Response vehicles had really slowed traffic.

"What's wrong?" Lexi asked Sha'qui. "You sound really upset."

"My cousin, Dori, just called me. She said Omar, Samson, and Edgar tried to hold up the Corner Mart tonight. She said Elle got shot, and," Sha'qui had to catch her breath, "and she's dead."

While Lexi listened to Sha'qui, Jonathan said something, and took off running toward the flashing police car lights. Now, Lexi became too weak to stand and the parking lot seemed to spin. She leaned against her car and tried to process what Sha'qui told her.

"Wait," Lexi said. "Are you sure? Is Dori sure?" Nothing seemed real. Lexi's pleasant evening with Jonathan had gone better than she ever expected. Now, Sha'qui had given her some of the worst news she could have gotten.

"I'm sure it's true," Sha'qui continued. "Pete and I are at Cancun Dunes and are on our way to you, but traffic is crazy. We're just across the road, but traffic is so bad Pete just turned to go to the light and turn around. We'll be where you are soon. Tell Jonathan we're on our way."

Lexi looked up and saw Jonathan across the parking lot. Tonight she had seen a strength in Jonathan that she didn't know he had. She had felt strangely safe with him while they ate and talked. Now, her world crumbled and she stood alone in the parking lot. It felt so dark and lonely here. The clouds hid the stars and moon. The security lights provided a strange orange kind of glow, but somehow it didn't seem like real light. Nothing seemed real right now except the feeling of betrayal and hurt. She really hoped she'd wake up and realize this had just been a dream.

Tears streamed down Lexi's face as she tried to sort out what Sha'qui had told her. Suddenly, Jonathan stood by her and said something to her, but she found herself unable to respond. Jonathan had a girl with him that Lexi didn't know. Lexi knew that she'd have a hard time telling Jonathan the news she'd from Sha'qui heard without getting very emotional. She didn't want to do that in front of someone she didn't know. Besides that, the girl with Jonathan had been crying and seemed to be very upset, or drunk. She seemed to be having trouble standing up. Lexi decided to wait for Sha'qui and Pete before she tried to talk. She didn't want to be the one to tell Jonathan.

Elle and Hannah had told Lexi they were doing something together tonight. What was it? Were they together? Had Sha'qui said anything about Hannah? Lexi looked up to see Jonathan talking to a woman who appeared to be the girl's mother. She and the girl soon left together, and Pete and Sha'qui arrived as they drove away.

Lexi thought the best thing for her to do would be to let Sha'qui and Pete tell Jonathan what they knew. She remained quiet and stayed at her car while they approached Jonathan. Pete seemed eager to talk to him.

After a minute or two, she heard Pete say to Jonathan, "Man, we gotta talk." He paused for a moment, then continued, "Someone did *try* to rob that store." Sha'qui leaned against Pete for support as he finished. "It was Edgar, Samson, and Omar."

"Oh, no!" Jonathan almost interrupted. "They told me they were going to do something to get money and that there was no way they were going to get caught. They even wanted me to join them. But I never dreamed..." He let the sentence go unfinished.

"Yeah," Pete replied, "they wanted me to go, too. They made it sound like they had a job or something. When I told them I had a date with Sha'qui, they laughed and walked off. I had no idea what they were planning. Sha'qui's cousin, Dori, called her a few minutes ago. She was there and saw some of it, then she heard Omar talking to one of the officers and got the rest of the story."

"And the robbery's not the bad part," Sha'qui said through tears. "It gets worse."

Pete continued his story. "Hannah and Elle started a fight out front to distract the attendant. When he went to see what was going on, Edgar, Samson, and Omar came in the back and were going to take the money from the office and the cash registers. They were supposed to be in and out in two minutes."

"Did they get hurt? Did they hurt someone?" Jonathan asked as quickly as he could talk.

"That's what Sha'qui was telling Lexi on the phone. Her cousin told her there were two people working," Pete continued, "but Edgar must have thought there would only be one. When they came in the back door, one of the attendants surprised them and they started shooting. We really don't know who shot first." Pete struggled to keep his composure and finish the story.

Jonathan looked at Lexi, who had her face buried in her hands as she leaned against her car. He started to step toward her but Pete continued.

"Omar, Edgar, and Samson didn't get hit and they didn't hit the attendants." Pete got choked up and couldn't finish. He didn't know that the attendants didn't even have guns.

The pieces of the puzzle came together in Jonathan's mind. If none of them got hit, and Chelsea said that a girl got shot… Jonathan felt a cold chill run through his whole body. He shivered and felt suddenly dizzy.

Pete tried to continue again, but couldn't for a minute. When he finally could, he started again. "Two of the shots that were fired at the attendants missed them, but they hit Elle and Hannah. Jonathan," Pete tried to continue, forcing himself to talk slowly to control his emotions, "they might both be dead, man. They might be dead."

Lexi stepped over and joined them. They all stood quietly for a few minutes before Pete could get composed enough to continue. "From what we were told, Elle got hit in the chest, and had a sheet over her. Hannah had blood all over her face and chest when they put her in the ambulance. We just don't know."

Sometimes, words are not strong enough to carry the message that needs to be communicated. Sometimes it requires holding someone's hand, or patting them on the back. Other times, a hug or a look through someone's eyes into their heart communicates better. Rain had stopped falling from the skies a few hours ago. Now, it fell from the eyes of grieving friends.

Chapter 17

Picking up the Pieces

Weeks later, Lexi hissed through her teeth as she reached out from under the covers to turn off her alarm clock. Somehow, she had forgotten to turn the alarm off last night. She had always treasured her weekend mornings because she could sleep late and rest.

Now, she loved sleeping late because she didn't feel the loss of her family while she slept. The day after Elle's funeral she had slept until 9:00, then she stayed in bed crying and grieving until almost noon. Today, Lexi turned the alarm clock off and tried to go back to sleep, but she couldn't. Her whole friend group really had seemed like family to her, and now that family had forever changed. The one part of her life she had counted on for stability had shattered.

Nothing in her life would be the same again. She lay in bed this morning tearfully thinking about her friends and these latest events. Elle would never again laugh and joke with them. One of the speakers at the funeral had talked about the time Elle spent in church as a child, and how much she had changed since she stopped attending. The look in the eyes of Elle's mother as she looked at Lexi and Sha'qui after the funeral broke both their hearts. She wouldn't speak to them. They had cried together as they wondered if Elle's mother blamed them for her death in some way.

Hannah had been released from the hospital into police custody because of her involvement in the robbery attempt. Lexi, Sha'qui, Pete, and Jonathan had tried to get permission to see her, but she said she didn't want to see anyone. She had told Lexi that the huge bandage on her face made her feel ugly, and that she hoped she could get the scar fixed even if she went to prison.

Omar, Edgar, and Samson hadn't been released from jail yet, and likely wouldn't be anytime soon. Jonathan and Pete had tried to visit them, but an attorney friend strongly advised them not to try right now. The fact that they had been friends, had spent a lot of time together, and had both been in trouble themselves might not "look good" he said. They told Lexi and Sha'qui what the attorney said, and they all decided to wait.

Lexi had talked briefly to Jonathan on the phone a few times since *that* night, but they hadn't spent much time face to face. She had relived the pleasant parts of their evening together many times. She watched the "memory movie" of the night again. She looked at his smile and his eyes, and listened to him laugh.

Since Jonathan had left the party life, Lexi had a growing desire to follow him. At first, she just wanted to be able to break out of the circle of behavior that seemed to have no destination. Then, she began to sense the desire to follow Jonathan more than just to leave the group and lifestyle. She began to miss the sounds and smells she associated with him. She didn't miss the smell of his cologne; she missed the smell of Jonathan. She couldn't describe it; she just missed it. She missed him.

During the week that everything had happened, Lexi had finally gathered up enough courage to ask Jonathan what made him change his life. She still didn't have all the answers she wanted to that question, but she didn't want to bother him. And she definitely didn't want him to feel as if she were chasing him. Jonathan seemed to have chosen a more settled life than the rest of their group. She wanted to know what he replaced everything with and how he had done it. How would her family group continue without one of the members? Would others leave, too?

Only one of those questions still needed an answer, because the whole family group had dissolved. None of their get-togethers or their parties would ever be the same. Still, she wondered about Jonathan. Although he obviously grieved the loss of his friends, he still seemed to be firmly grounded in something. Whatever had helped him to change his life seemed to be helping him deal with all the stresses he faced now. Whatever it was, she wanted it, too.

As Lexi got out of the bed she made sure her alarm clock didn't come on again. Her phone sat on the bathroom counter, charging. When she went to get it, she found a text from Jonathan.

"Text me when you get a chance. I got you one of the books I told you about. We can get together sometime soon and work on it, if you're still interested."

Lexi's heart jumped. "Of course I'm still interested," she said to her reflection in the mirror. She immediately sent a text back to Jonathan.

Within a few seconds, her phone rang. Caller ID told her Jonathan had decided to call instead of texting.

"Good morning," she said as she smiled and winked at her reflection.

"Good morning," Jonathan replied. His voice sounded light and full of energy. Lexi imagined him smiling. "I got the workbook I told you about if you're still interested in watching the video with me. I mean, you can do it yourself, if you want to, but –"

"No!" Lexi interrupted, "I'd like to watch it with you. Especially since you've already been through it. Would you like to watch it here?" Lexi hoped she didn't sound too eager, but she knew her excitement showed in her voice.

"That's fine with me," Jonathan answered. "When do you want to get together?"

"The sooner, the better for me. This evening, if you want," she replied. "I'm feeling kinda scattered since, well you know."

"Yeah, I know," Jonathan agreed. "Me, too. I've been talking to Jimmy and Angie some. They've helped me a lot. I've also been praying and going to church some, but it's kinda lonely when you don't know anyone there. They're really friendly, and I like it, but still."

"I totally understand," Lexi said. "I've been talking to some of the ladies from work. This is all so hard. I can't believe Elle is gone, and our whole group is scattered out now."

"Yep," Jonathan said, sounding a little harsh. Then he continued more softly, "I know what you mean. Hey, since we're watching at your house, what time do you want me there? I'm off today, and I feel cooped up. I need to get out of here."

"Sure," Lexi responded immediately. "What about five o'clock? And I'll fix us some dinner. Didn't you say the video stuff is in sections?"

"Yeah, we'll be able to take a break after each section. They'll only take a few minutes each." Lexi smiled. She knew that they were both using the DVD and book as an excuse to see one another for a no-pressure date.

"Oh," Jonathan added, "I'll have to tell you what Uncle Steve talked to me about this week, too."

"Okay," Lexi replied excitedly. "I can't wait. I have to go to the store today, so I'll see you this evening." She also wanted to clean up some, but she didn't tell him that part.

"See you then!" Jonathan replied.

Lexi set her phone on the counter and started getting ready to go to the store. Suddenly, the whole day seemed much brighter.

*   *   *

Jonathan sat for a minute after he finished talking to Lexi. He watched some birds in his back yard while he drank the last bit of his coffee. He finished his cereal and started thinking about what to do with the rest of his day. A knock on the front door interrupted his planning.

When Jonathan opened the door, he fully expected to see someone selling something. Cookies, newspapers, new cable services – someone was always selling something. Today, no salesman had knocked. Instead, Jonathan opened the door to find a red-haired man standing there holding a small notebook. He looked professional, but casual at the same time. He almost looked like a detective, but somehow different.

"Jonathan Timms?" the man asked in a tone that assumed he was right.

"Yes," Jonathan hesitated as he answered.

"I'm Kyle Alan, the head of Tri-Central Probation." Jonathan started to say something, but Mr. Alan didn't give him time to respond. "And before you tell me that you're not on probation anymore, I already know that. That's not why I'm here. This is a sort of a personal visit. Do you have time to talk for a minute?"

"Sure." Jonathan tried to hide the look of absolute confusion that he felt. Probation officers had checked on him before, but never their head person. When they had come, it usually meant they were checking him for drugs, or to have him arrested for some probation violation. Jonathan decided to invite him in to talk. "Come on in."

Jonathan moved some papers out of the chair and off the sofa in his living room. Then, he motioned to Mr. Alan to have a seat.

"Mr. Timms," Mr. Alan began, "I've known who you were for several months, but I don't think you know me. You've been on probation with our office a couple of times, and I've seen you in the office, but we've never talked. I saw you in the jail the last time you were arrested."

"I remember that," Jonathan said. "And I've seen you around some since then."

"I would imagine you have," Mr. Alan laughed. "Let me tell you why I'm here, and let me say again that you're not in trouble, so you can relax."

"I didn't think I was in trouble. I've been making a lot of changes," Jonathan interjected. "Does this have anything to do with my friends and the Corner Mart stuff that happened?"

"Not exactly," Mr. Alan replied. "Several months ago you were working on the building site next door to my house. You were digging footers for a house, and you were also working on leveling a parking space. For about two weeks you worked on a tractor and then on a backhoe. It was in the old Carter subdivision. Do you remember it?"

"I sure do," Jonathan nodded. "It was so hot and dusty!"

"Do you remember a little boy sitting in a tree on the lot next door and watching you?" Mr. Alan asked.

Jonathan did remember the little boy, and they had waved at one another a couple of times. "I do," Jonathan said.

"Well, that's my son. He watched you every day that you were there. Several times he has pointed you out when we rode by your worksites. Sometimes he points you out in restaurants or stores. You've become quite a hero to him. He says he wants to be like you when he grows up. He wants to drive a backhoe."

Jonathan didn't know what to say. He had never thought about anyone wanting to be like him. Jonathan remembered being high at least part of one of the days during the time the little boy had started watching him. The thought of a little boy wanting to drive a backhoe when he grew up made sense to Jonathan. The thought of a little boy wanting to be like him, especially the way he'd been then, bothered him beyond words.

"I never knew anyone watched me, especially to look up to me,"

Jonathan said. "The Jonathan that I was then is certainly not someone you want your son to be like."

"Yeah, I know," Mr. Alan said simply. "I'm also a volunteer for a wilderness scouting group for teenage boys. Some of them come from high-risk backgrounds and have no strong male role models in their lives. A few of them know you, and have talked to my son about you. They all think it would be cool to drink beer like you do, and drive backhoes for a living. One of the boys even talked about dropping out of school because you don't need a diploma to drive a backhoe." Mr. Alan paused for Jonathan to think.

For the first time, Jonathan realized that his actions had caused a ripple effect in his community. Not only did his life affect him and his close friends, but it affected people that he didn't even know. He thought about Elle and how she admired and looked up to Omar. He remembered her funeral. He thought about Robert sitting in the recliner in his drunken stupor holding his beer. Then he thought about the boys who thought it would be cool to hold their beer and drive a backhoe. Could it be possible that he, Jonathan Timms, was leading those boys to become like Robert?

"You see, Mr. Timms," Mr. Alan said, "these boys don't see what you think you're doing, or even what you really are doing. They see what *they* think you're doing."

Jonathan almost felt sick. With all his heart he wanted to change. He had changed and was still changing. But what had he done to those boys? To what future had he led them? What about other boys or even girls had he influenced that he didn't know about?

Mr. Alan continued, suddenly sounding much more personal, "Jonathan, I'm not here to condemn you or to complain. I have seen huge changes in you in the last few weeks. What I'm here for today is to ask you if you'd consider volunteering with me on the weekends to work with these boys, and let them get to know you like you are now. I want them to know the real you! I think it would be good for you and good for them. I guess what I'm asking is this. How would you like to pour your life into some boys?"

Jonathan didn't know what to say. Mr. Alan actually sat here and offered him the opportunity to undo some of the things he had done wrong. For a minute, Jonathan found himself too shocked to answer.

Mr. Alan continued. "I've talked to Jimmy Betts, Mr. Steve Green, and your old probation officers. They all agree that you have a lot to offer, and that I'm not wasting my time or endangering the boys. Until you've worked closely with me for about a year, until you've proven yourself, you won't be alone with the boys. You'll be working directly under me. But you'll have a chance to make a difference." Mr. Alan waited for Jonathan to think things through.

"Mr. Alan, several weeks ago Jimmy Betts talked to me for a long time. He helped me realize that my life was full of mistakes and that I had been too hardheaded to change. He offered to pour his life into me, as long as I didn't turn my cup upside down and waste it. Until then, I was literally breached, broken, and bottom up. Now you're asking me to pour into these boys what has been poured into me. My answer is *Yes, sir!*" He reached his hand out to shake Mr. Alan's and found a firm and eager hand waiting.

"I'm so glad! You have no idea how much these boys admire you. You really have a chance to make a difference here. Just be sure you don't lead them the wrong way. Here's my number and contact information. Is it okay if I call you next week and we work out when you can meet with us?" he asked as he handed Jonathan a business card.

"It sure is," Jonathan answered. "And here's my card," he said as he handed Mr. Alan his own business card. "My uncle just made me a junior partner in his business this week and had these made up for me."

"Awesome," Mr. Alan said with a smile as he took the card and started for the door. "This has been a great visit, but I have to go. Thank you for your willingness to help."

"Thank you for the opportunity," Jonathan said, returning the smile.

"I'll call you next week," Mr. Alan said as he went to his car.

Jonathan waved briefly as he remembered the last time someone had come and offered him an opportunity. Omar and Mr. Alan had offered him such different choices. He debated whether he'd share all of this with Lexi when they got together. So many changes were happening in his life right now. He hoped they would all turn out for the good.

Just this week, Uncle Steve had told him that he wanted to work less and have Jonathan take over more responsibilities. He planned to train

Jonathan to take over the company eventually. He'd already had business cards printed for Jonathan when he asked him about it. At first, Jonathan had refused, but later decided he'd like the challenge. Then, he got excited and wanted to share the news.

When he called his mother to tell her about it, he found that Uncle Steve had already told her. Good news always tastes better when you share it with someone who doesn't already know. He decided the only one close enough to share with, and who didn't already know, would be Lexi. Since Mr. Alan came by, Jonathan had two things he wanted to share with her.

Chapter 18

Sum it Up

As Jonathan drove to Lexi's house, his mind overflowed with thoughts. His whole life had changed in just a few months. So much had happened to him in just the last couple of weeks. He decided not to try to talk to Lexi about the changes and opportunities in his life all at once. He would just spend time with her and enjoy the evening. He hoped she'd like the video and that it would help her as much as it had helped him. He even decided that he'd send a book and DVD to Ashleigh if Lexi liked it.

The car in front of him slowed to turn in at a restaurant. He recognized it as Pete's car and he saw Pete and Sha'qui waving at him. They were on a date again. Jonathan had a few minutes, so he pulled in behind them to say hello and visit for a minute. When Pete and Sha'qui got out of their car, Jonathan pulled up close and let down his window.

"Hey, man, what's up?" he asked Pete through the open window.

"Hey, man!" Pete answered. "We're about to take advantage of wing night, then we might catch a movie. What about you?"

"I'm on my way to Lexi's house. She's cooking something and then we're going to watch a video and work on this *Castles of Character* book I bought. It has helped me a lot and she wants to do it, too." Jonathan's answer almost sounded rehearsed, even to him.

Pete looked at Sha'qui, then back at Jonathan. "So, you're just going to work on some workbook, but she's cooking for you?"

"Yes," Jonathan answered simply.

Pete looked at Sha'qui again, and his smile got bigger. "Have you ever

164

had her cooking before?" Pete asked. He sounded like he had a follow-up comment ready.

"Well, no," Jonathan admitted. "She just offered to cook."

"I've had her cooking before," Pete said as he looked at Sha'qui and winked. "If she's cooking for you, and cooking at her house, you're gonna be eating some husband-bait in just a little while."

Jonathan laughed. "I really don't think that's what she has on her mind," Jonathan started, but Pete interrupted.

"That ain't what I mean, man. Once you eat some of her cooking, that's what's going to be on *your* mind. That woman can cook!" Pete said, and he and Sha'qui laughed together.

"Well, I'll let you know about all that later," Jonathan said as he joined their laughter. Suddenly he felt a little uncomfortable with the conversation. "I'll see you later," he said as he drove away.

As he drove off, he found himself grateful for the healing that he saw in Pete and Sha'qui, and for the healing he felt. He felt a twinge of pain for his other friends and the tremendous loss they all experienced. *That* night had hurt so many people. Still, they had to go on with their lives.

Jonathan remembered what Mr. Alan had told him about the boys that were watching him. He wondered how many lives had been affected by the robbery and shooting. He knew about some of those lives and how they'd been affected, but how many did he *not* know about? How many would follow Omar or Samson or Edgar as heroes and want to have shootouts at convenience stores? How many young boys had they led to prison without even thinking? Jonathan tried to put all of these thoughts out of his mind as he pulled up into the driveway in front of Lexi's door.

He knocked on the door just before 5:00. He had decided not to let all of his recent distractions become the topic of conversation tonight. He tried to bury all of his personal feelings and just focus on the evening. He didn't want to seem like he had come just to bore her with his life.

"Come in!" she invited as she opened the door wide. "The food is almost ready."

Jonathan smelled something cooking. The smell, the lighting, and the look on Lexi's face told him he could relax. At least for this evening, and right here, he could let his guard down and feel at home. He needed someone to talk to, and he began to feel like he could talk to her.

"That smells so good!" Jonathan said. "I didn't think I was very hungry, but, wow!"

"Thank you!" Lexi said as she smiled. "It's just spaghetti and garlic bread."

"When you're a guy and you live alone, there's no such thing as 'just spaghetti' unless it comes cold out of a can. And I can tell that didn't." He smiled as he looked at her, then past her to the kitchen.

Lexi led him to the table, and said, "I really miss having adult conversations, since I live alone. While we eat, would you tell me all about what's going on in the life of Jonathan?"

"You don't want to hear all my boring junk," he answered as he sat down in the chair she offered.

"It might not be boring to me," she replied as she got plates and went to the stove. "I'll tell you what, you tell me the boring stuff, and I'll let you know if I get bored. Fair enough?" Her genuine interest seemed to make Jonathan want to talk.

Lexi drained the spaghetti noodles, stirred the sauce, and placed bread on the plates. Jonathan began to tell her about his work. At first he talked about the new backhoe and the worksites. As she got their tea and water ready, he began to talk about Jimmy and Angie. Then, Lexi sat down and patiently waited for him to pause. In a couple of minutes, he grew quiet.

"When we ate together last time, you told me you liked to pray before you eat. Would you do that again?" Lexi gently asked.

Jonathan couldn't hide his surprise, or his delight. "I'll be glad to, if you want," he said. After she nodded, he prayed, "Great God, thank you for this food, and for a friend like Lexi. And for what you're doing for me, uh, for us. Amen."

"May I ask what God is doing for you? You seem to be changing, and you started telling me about it a little, but I'm really interested. Is it private, or can you tell me?" Lexi asked.

"I'd be glad to share," Jonathan said between mouthfuls. "You see; I know this girl who makes this great spaghetti." He teased as he put another forkful in his mouth and smiled. After he swallowed, he continued with a more serious tone. "You remember that night when I got drunk and blew up at Katie?" Lexi nodded, and he continued, "Well, then I went on that anger rant, and I woke up in jail. When I realized what the alcohol and drugs had cost me, I was disgusted."

Jonathan went on for an hour, telling Lexi all about the jail and his visits with Jimmy and Angie. Then he told her about Ashleigh and how broken she had been. He went in great detail about how he felt like he met himself in Robert's living room. He told her how sick and disgusted he felt when he heard his own words coming from Robert's drunken mouth. He told her about Ashleigh's visit with Aunt Jo, and Ashleigh going into treatment. Then he told her about the Bible verses Jimmy had given him. He seemed to get a little emotional when he told her about his experience with the Bible that Emilie had given him and his prayer time with God that night.

"I really stopped being the old me and started being a new me when I prayed that night," Jonathan confessed. "I know it doesn't make sense, but the old Jonathan died in that chair that night, and a new one was born. I became a new person. Now, I'm trying to learn to live like a new person." The fullness of what he had in his mind couldn't be formed into words. He struggled to continue, then just paused, hoping she would understand what he couldn't say.

When he paused for a minute, Lexi seemed to sense that he had run out of words. She stood slowly and touched him on the shoulder briefly as she took the opportunity to clear away their dishes. She put the dishes into the dishwasher and started to wipe the table and stove.

While she did the quick clean, Jonathan stood up slowly. He wiped his hands on a napkin and moved toward the sofa where the DVD and workbook lay. Lexi followed close behind him. Then he told Lexi about his day of working on the video and workbook.

"It made me take a close look at myself and the decisions I'd made and the ones I still needed to make. It really helped me. I think it also helped me know how to organize the things I needed to do, and still need to do, in my new life with God. Even Uncle Steve noticed that I've changed, and he made me a junior partner in the business. He wants me to eventually run the company. It's made me think about my future a lot more, settling down maybe," Jonathan stopped cold. He suddenly realized how close to a marriage proposal this might sound!

He recovered quickly and nervously continued, trying to refocus the conversation back to the video. "I still have a lot to figure out. I'm looking forward to doing the video and workbook again," he said.

"I'm looking forward to it, too," Lexi said. Before she could finish her thought, he continued.

"One reason I think it's so important to me is something that happened today," Jonathan turned toward her. "The new head of the probation company, Mr. Kyle Alan, came by today to talk to me."

"I didn't think you were on probation anymore," Lexi said as she stopped and faced him. He could see the concern showing in her eyes.

"I'm not. At least, I'm not on that kind of probation," Jonathan replied and looked suddenly very thoughtful. "And, then again, I'll always be on probation, I guess."

Lexi sat down with her legs crossed under her and faced Jonathan. "I don't understand," she said simply. Her tone begged for more information, but she didn't ask.

"The short version is that his son and some other boys had been talking and had kind of a 'Jonathan fan club' going on. The problem is, they were fans of the old Jonathan, and were idolizing me drinking a beer and driving a backhoe. Which," he looked Lexi straight in the eyes and said bluntly, "I have never done at the same time. Mr. Alan made a good point when he said that the boys were following what they thought they had seen, not necessarily what I had really done." He paused for a moment struggling with the reality of what he was saying.

He continued, "One of the boys even talked about dropping out of school because he wouldn't need to finish school to be like me. It made me realize that I've been leading a lot of people in the wrong direction. Then he asked me to come and help him with the scouting group he leads and help teach the boys good values. I can kinda undo the bad I had started in the boys' lives."

Jonathan's desire to be a good, solid man seemed to really touch Lexi. She shifted her weight and focused her gaze on him as if she were getting ready to say something very serious.

"I don't know if you realize it, but you've been leading me for a while, now," she said as she looked into his eyes. "You've been showing me how to change, and leading me toward a life in God. That's something I've never had, or even thought about. You'll be great with the boys."

A gentle, almost happy, beeping sound made Lexi look toward the kitchen. Jonathan suddenly became aware of a wonderful, sweet smell. Lexi stood up and started toward the oven while pointing toward the DVD player.

"If you'll get the video ready, I'll get the brownies ready," she said with a playful smile. "I thought we could concentrate better if we had a little treat for our breaks. If they're ready, they should be cool enough to eat in just a few minutes."

While Jonathan started getting the video and workbook ready, he had a thought. He spoke loud enough for her to hear him from the kitchen. "If you like the video and think it would be a good idea, I'm thinking about sending one to my friend Ashleigh. She's in a long term drug and alcohol rehab center. She seems to be doing great, but this might help her, too."

"Makes sense," Lexi said. "I know *I* can use it."

"How much do you want to try to do each time?" he asked Lexi. "I went through all of this in about two or three days, but I worked straight through. Doing the sessions with someone else, it might take longer. If we take our time and talk about these sessions, and don't try to rush, we might only do one session a week. That could take a while, though. There are 12 sessions."

Lexi continued working at the table in the kitchen and answered over her shoulder. "It's totally up to you. We can do several sessions this weekend, if you want."

She returned from the kitchen and put a huge plate of brownies on the small table in front of Jonathan. Then, she went to the kitchen and returned with a large glass of milk that she handed him.

"I was thinking about going to church tomorrow," Jonathan said. "So I can't do a marathon on the video *this* weekend." He reached for a brownie. He hoped that she'd take the hint and would want to get together again, maybe even next weekend.

"That's fine," she answered simply. "I might go to church tomorrow, too." She paused and watched Jonathan picking up his brownie.

Jonathan put the brownie in his mouth. *OH, WOW!* His eyes half closed, and he almost felt like he floated off the sofa for a second. Suddenly, Pete's words began to echo in his head, and Jonathan looked at the plate of brownies. Definite husband-bait, he thought, and he realized Lexi was talking.

"But if you want to take it slowly, and do one session each week," her eyes met his and she looked thoughtfully at him, "I don't have any other plans for the next 12 weekends."

CPSIA information can be obtained
at www.ICGtesting.com
Printed in the USA
JSHW021502300520
5962JS00001B/1